"I know you don't want to upset anyone."

Palmer went on, "I think you need to take that DNA test. And tomorrow, when I talk to some of the nurses who worked at the hospital when you were born, you should come with."

"If they're local..." Louisa started.

"I know. Gossip is inevitable. But this is dangerous. What's more important? Sparing your parents' feelings? Or keeping you all safe? Order the test. Come with me to talk to the nurses. If we think they can't keep quiet, we'll warn your parents ahead of time."

It sounded terrible. Except one part. "'We'?"

"You dragged me into this, Lou. You aren't kicking me back out."

"People are going to start talking. If they haven't already. About us spending all this time together."

"Yeah, they are."

He took her hand. Then he pulled her closer.

And closer.

"What are you doing?" she asked.

"What I've been promising myself I wouldn't do since you came home from college."

Then his mouth was on hers.

COLD CASE
IDENTITY

—

NICOLE HELM

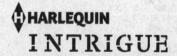

For the "bad boy/good man" heroes.

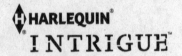

HARLEQUIN®
INTRIGUE™

ISBN-13: 978-1-335-59066-4

Cold Case Identity

Copyright © 2024 by Nicole Helm

Recycling programs
for this product may
not exist in your area.

For questions and comments about the quality of this book,
please contact us at CustomerService@Harlequin.com.

Harlequin Enterprises ULC
22 Adelaide St. West, 41st Floor
Toronto, Ontario M5H 4E3, Canada
www.Harlequin.com

Printed in U.S.A.

Nicole Helm grew up with her nose in a book and the dream of one day becoming a writer. Luckily, after a few failed career choices, she gets to follow that dream—writing down-to-earth contemporary romance and romantic suspense. From farmers to cowboys, Midwest to *the* West, Nicole writes stories about people finding themselves and finding love in the process. She lives in Missouri with her husband and two sons, and dreams of someday owning a barn.

Books by Nicole Helm

Harlequin Intrigue

Hudson Sibling Solutions

Cold Case Kidnapping
Cold Case Identity

Covert Cowboy Soldiers

The Lost Hart Triplet
Small Town Vanishing
One Night Standoff
Shot in the Dark
Casing the Copycat
Clandestine Baby

A North Star Novel Series

Summer Stalker
Shot Through the Heart
Mountainside Murder
Cowboy in the Crosshairs
Dodging Bullets in Blue Valley
Undercover Rescue

Visit the Author Profile page at Harlequin.com.

CAST OF CHARACTERS

Palmer Hudson—Part-time rancher and part-time investigator for Hudson Sibling Solutions, a cold case investigation business run from the family's ranch. Used to be in the rodeo. Currently helping his little sister's best friend look into a family mystery.

Louisa O'Brien—Helps run her family orchard and has recently discovered that she may have been stolen as a baby. Wants Palmer to help her find the truth without anyone finding out. Has been in love with Palmer since she was a teenager.

Kyla Brown—The woman who messaged Louisa about the possibility she might be the baby who was stolen years ago. She is the stolen baby's sister.

Anna Hudson—Palmer's youngest sister and Louisa's best friend since they were kids.

Jack, Cash, Mary and Grant Hudson—Palmer's siblings, who also help run the ranch and Hudson Sibling Solutions.

Izzy Hudson—Palmer's niece.

Dahlia Easton—Grant's girlfriend, a librarian in town.

The O'Brien family—Tim and Minnie, Louisa's parents; Greg, Louisa's grandfather. All live on and help run the family orchard.

Hawk Steele—The fire investigator who gets involved in the case through a fire at the O'Brien orchard.

Chapter One

Palmer Hudson liked to have fun. He'd learned at an early age that life was going to punch you in the nose as often as it could, so you might as well enjoy the ride between blows.

That didn't mean he was irresponsible. Maybe, on occasion, he hit the bottle a little harder than he should, and definitely, on occasion, he was a little careless with women, but always, no matter what, Palmer showed up and did what he was tasked with doing.

Some days, it was ranch chores at the sprawling Hudson Ranch, which had been part of his family for five generations. And sometimes it was stepping in as investigator on one of the cold cases his family investigated as part of Hudson Sibling Solutions—his oldest brother's brainchild after the disappearance of their parents when Palmer had been twelve.

One day they'd been there…and then they'd been gone.

No one had ever figured out what had happened to them. But Jack had stepped up and taken care of the five minor Hudson kids. Jack had been eighteen and had taken on the weight of *everything*.

Had it turned him into an uptight tool most days? In Palmer's estimation, yes. He could hardly hold it against Jack when Jack had kept them together. Driven him to football practices, signed off on his joining the rodeo early, made sure there was food in the fridge and money in the bank.

Jack had been the glue so much so that, even though they'd each tried their hand at off-ranch things—Grant had joined the marines for a time, Cash had gotten married and had a kid, Mary had gone to college and Anna had tried her own brief stint at the rodeo—all these years later, they were all back home. At the Hudson Ranch. Running Hudson Sibling Solutions and living just outside the Sunrise town limits.

Family.

Nearing thirty, Palmer didn't consider his wild days behind him, but he supposed he was starting to understand the adult art of *balance*.

Mostly, he thought darkly when he recognized the raven-haired woman sauntering toward him. He'd been heading for the main house, but now he was seriously considering turning on a heel and beating a hasty retreat.

Louisa O'Brien was the one person, maybe in the whole world, who made Palmer Hudson *uncomfortable*.

Since she was his kid sister's best friend, he'd once enjoyed annoying and torturing Anna and Louisa whenever given the opportunity. It's what big brothers were for.

But ever since Louisa had come home from some fancy college out east a couple of years back, Palmer had done his level best to steer clear.

Because Louisa O'Brien had grown up into a flat-out knockout. Wavy black hair that she almost always hung loose around her shoulders, dark green eyes the color of deep summer and an almost-constant smirk that promised she knew a lot more than you did. Not to mention the way she wore her jeans—which he absolutely refused to notice ever since that *one* time he had very much *not* realized it was Louisa he'd been ogling at the local bar.

He might not have a lot of boundaries when it came to women, but Louisa was one.

"Hey, Palmer," she greeted, coming to a stop in front of him.

He hadn't run away, so he supposed he just had to deal. Much as it pained him. "Afternoon, Louisa. Anna's out of town."

"Yeah, I know. I actually came by to see you."

"What the hell for?" That was another thing about adult Louisa. He was forever saying the wrong thing around her when he'd never had trouble charming a woman in his entire life. From the *cradle*, he'd been able to wrap the female population around his...finger.

Of course, he didn't want to charm Louisa. He wanted to stay the hell away from her at any and all costs.

She grinned at him, green eyes wreaking real havoc with his system—a system that should absolutely know better.

"I need a favor," she said, and though she tried to keep the grin stretched wide, he saw the shift in her eyes. Something serious lurked behind that attempt at amusement.

"Why don't you ask literally anyone else?"

"Why so grumpy?" she asked, reaching out to poke his chest.

He sidestepped her. He had learned that *nothing* good came from pretending like she didn't affect him. So, he just straight up *avoided*.

"Got things to do, Louisa."

"And people, I assume," she returned with a smirk. A smirk with *just* enough flirtation that he had to very firmly take his imagination to task. No picturing Louisa O'Brien in absolute any kind of state of undress.

Ever.

"I need shady help," she said, as if she didn't know how she affected him when he had the sneaking suspicion she knew and used it against him. Routinely. "And you're the shady one."

"Anna's shady."

"No, Anna's vengeful," she corrected. "There's a difference."

It was true, but Palmer didn't have to like it.

"It's a bit delicate. I'd ask Cash, but he's not taking cases right now. At least, that's what Mary said. And as much as I trust Anna with anything... Well, I need a delicate hand."

It irritated him that she'd want to go to Cash over him, which wasn't a fair assessment since he didn't want her coming to him. But still. Emotions and facts didn't always line up neatly. So, his response was a little gruffer than it should have been. "Since when is that my department?"

She blew a breath, frowning out over the distant mountains. Something twisted in his stomach. He very much wanted to fix whatever was worrying her. But he could not take that risk.

When she returned her gaze to him, he was sunk. "This is serious, and I need someone I can trust. I'd go to Grant or Jack, but they're just too...straight and narrow. I need someone who's not afraid to bend the law a little. I need answers at literally *any* cost."

"*Any* cost is a dangerous proposition, Louisa. You might want to rethink what you're offering." Because every now and again, the best defense was an obnoxious offense.

She frowned. "No one's paying you to be a jerk."

"Nope, I do it for free since I love it so much."

She laughed. That was another problem with Louisa. Sure, like everyone else, she didn't take him too seriously, but she didn't get bent out of shape. She took things as they came, and since that was his entire life motto, he couldn't help but respect it.

Her laugh died quickly though, and any attempt at humor too. She clasped her hands together, looking up at him imploringly.

Hell and damn.

"I found something that changes my entire life, Palmer. I need answers. I need help. I don't know who else to go to."

"Like what?"

"Like... I don't think my parents are who they say they are. I don't think I'm theirs. And I don't think any of it was ever legal."

LOUISA WOULDN'T CRY in front of Palmer Hudson for a million dollars. She had pride. Some people had told her she had too much.

She didn't mind. Pride got a person places,

and it kept them protected from people taking advantage. It protected soft hearts that didn't want to be soft.

So, she had her pride and she forced back every last *drop* of moisture in her eyes that threatened. Even though it was hard.

She'd never said the words she'd just uttered out loud to Palmer or *anyone*. She still didn't want to believe it. But the past six months had her feeling hollowed out and empty. Sad and scared. She couldn't live in denial any longer. She needed answers.

She hoped to *God* she got answers that were comfortable. With every passing month, it felt less and less likely.

"I don't follow," Palmer said, studying her in that careful way of his. Palmer played into his fun-loving, heavy-drinking, serial-dating rep-utation. He made sure everyone thought there wasn't much substance under that black cow-boy hat.

But Louisa knew his family saw the sub-stance underneath, and she knew that under all those bad boy ways he'd learned to cope with his parents' disappearance was a man who was careful with the things that mattered.

She wasn't ashamed to admit, in the privacy of her own mind, that she'd been in love with Palmer Hudson since she was thirteen years old.

Who would have been able to resist? He'd been impressive at seventeen. Homecoming king. Football quarterback. Off to the rodeo, always smiling and laughing despite the tragedy that had befallen his family.

She'd believed—hoped—for years she'd grow out of those feelings for him. She knew he'd never, *ever* reciprocate those feelings. But hers stubbornly and religiously stayed, even after her four-year stint in New England for college.

Even if she sometimes entertained the fantasy he might reciprocate *other* things if not feelings.

Regardless, she loved him. And she'd bite her own tongue off before she admitted it to anyone.

That little wrinkle had kept her from asking for his help for months now. She'd tried to think of a way to bring it up to Anna that wouldn't send Anna flying off the handle. She'd considered, over and over again, consulting one of the other Hudsons. *Any* other Hudson.

But if everything she suspected was true, *she* was a cold case. And she needed help. Careful help. Determined help.

Palmer fit the bill. Unfortunately, more than anyone else. He wouldn't want revenge. He wouldn't tell anyone. He wouldn't follow every law to the letter.

He'd find her answers.

Maybe he'd tempt her in the process. Because, damn, the man was enticing. If that was the price she had to pay, then so be it.

"So, this woman found me on Facebook," she said, since starting at the very beginning seemed safer somehow.

"No reasonable story starts with those words, Lou." He looked down at her, so condescending, she almost turned and left right then and there. She didn't need his disdain. She didn't need *him*.

But she did need answers.

"She was a freshman at my alma matter," Louisa continued, trying to keep the snap out of her tone. "And she'd seen my softball team photo in the athletic complex from when we won our championship."

"Still proud of that one, huh?"

"I assume you're still proud of all your buckles?"

He didn't respond to that.

"So, she contacts you and says what?"

"That we're identical. And isn't that so weird? She sent me her softball picture."

"You opened an attachment from an unknown source?"

"Yeah, I did, Palmer. So buy me some antivirus software. The point is, she was right. She looked almost exactly the same as I did at eighteen. We decided to try to trace our family trees to see if we…connected somehow. Like long-lost identical cousins."

"And you didn't?"

"No. But then she suggested we do one of those ancestry DNA tests. You know? The ones that tell you where your family came from, and you can connect to other people with the same DNA or whatever."

"Sure."

"I was kind of excited. I thought it would be something cool. Like my great-great-grandma had an affair with some outlaw. I thought it would be fun, maybe funny. I entertained the possibility we weren't related at all and we're just freak doppelgangers too, but dreaming up how we might connect felt… I don't know. It was just *fun*. So I told my parents. I thought we should all do it."

He must have read something in her tone because his frown deepened. "They didn't go for it?"

"They forbid me."

Palmer's eyebrows drew together. "Forbid you? I didn't think your parents forbid you *anything*."

"Well, I wouldn't go *that* far, but no. They've always been lenient. Bent over backward to make me happy. I know that." She wrapped her arms around herself. It was silly. A silly thing to still be upset about, but it was *jarring* when parents got really militantly angry for the first time when you were *twenty-four*.

Even when they'd caught her with a beer after graduation, she'd gotten gentle talking-tos, despite every don't-drink-before-you're-legal lecture known to man. They just…didn't get mad. They were overprotective, but they were careful.

Now she wanted to know why. Why for twenty-four years they'd been so accommodating when all her friends had had more rules, more lectures, angry fights with their parents as they'd experimented with teenage rebellion.

But Louisa had never been able to rebel, even when she'd tried, because her parents did not forbid.

Until, as an adult, she'd asked to do a fun little DNA test. "They threw a whole fit. Said it was dangerous to give your DNA to those places and there was no way any of *our* DNA was going to be sent off to some shady business."

"It's not a bad point, Louisa."

She didn't groan, though she badly wanted to. "No, it wasn't. Still, I wouldn't have thought anything of it. If they'd been rational. If this woman hadn't told me…"

"Told you what?" Palmer asked.

This was the hard part. The part that didn't make any sense. The part that, for months, she had convinced herself wasn't true. Until Kyla Brown from Lakely, Ohio, had sent her picture after picture of family members who looked like Louisa herself.

When she'd never once been told she took after her parents. Never *once*.

"Her older sister was stolen as a baby. Kidnapped. They never found her—not a baby or a body. And they never figured out who did it."

"Louisa. You can't be serious." He didn't sound condescending this time. No, he sounded like he *pitied* her.

That was worse.

"I know it sounds out there. I want it to be a lie. A joke." She had to pause to swallow the emotion that threatened to envelope her whole. She'd been trying to deny it for so long, but she simply couldn't any longer. "I so desperately want it to be a bizarre coincidence. That's why I need help. Someone who can be…impartial. Who can find the answers at *any* cost. And who can keep a secret while I try to find answers."

Palmer didn't say anything at first. Louisa hugged herself tighter. The air had gotten colder, the wind picking up, likely blowing in a storm.

Palmer frowned then shrugged off his coat and settled it on her shoulders over her jacket, which wasn't doing its job.

"Storm blowing in," he muttered. "Come on inside for dinner. We'll sort it out from there."

That was not a no.

But it was the first step into finding out if she was really...who she thought she was. If her parents were good, honest people. Or liars and kidnappers.

Louisa let out a shaky breath as she followed him to the Hudsons' sprawling house, the warmth of his coat trying valiantly to chase the chill from her bones.

It was no use. None of this felt good or right, but having Palmer agree to help was a step.

They'd find the truth. Then she'd figure out how to deal with it.

Chapter Two

"You can't tell anyone," Louisa said before he pulled open the front door to the house he'd spent most of his life in. "I need this to be a secret."

He looked down at her. She only came to about his chin. The Hudson boys had been blessed with their father's height and, as their mother had liked to say, *his* father's hard head.

God, he missed his mother at the oddest times. Like walking into Hudson house with little Louisa O'Brien at his side needing help.

"We'll eat and then we'll talk," Palmer replied. He didn't need to lead Louisa to the dining room. She'd attended quite a few dinners here growing up. He remembered one memorable one, before his parents had gone missing, where Anna and Louisa had insisted on acting like dogs for the whole of the meal.

The only thing that had kept Palmer from partaking had been the potential teasing he would have gotten from his older brothers for joining in with the *babies*.

He missed having those sorts of problems now too. Those were simple problems.

But what had been simple since that fateful day when he'd been twelve?

Booze. Bulls. Women.

He sighed inwardly. But *not* Louisa.

The dining room was already full. Cash and his daughter, Izzy, were giving their menagerie of dogs orders. Jack was seated at the head of the table reading on his phone and Mary was putting the finishing touches on dinner with Dahlia's help. Dahlia was the one new addition to the house, ever since she'd had the bad taste to fall for Grant when they'd taken on her case last month.

When Mary looked up and saw them, she smiled. Ever the hostess. "Oh, Louisa. Anna isn't here. She got held up out of town. But come on in. You can eat her portion."

"Thanks, Mary."

"Just *where* has Anna been held up?" Jack asked darkly, putting his phone down on the table—screen up. Sometimes he looked so much like their father, it felt like Palmer had been shoved into a strange dream where his father was alive and well and right there.

But Jack wasn't their father, so no one really

answered him about Anna's mysterious where-abouts. Anna had gone out and gotten her private investigator's license a few years ago and sometimes took on jobs outside Hudson Sibling Solutions. Mostly to make Jack angry.

It had worked.

"How's the orchard business?" Cash asked Louisa after the silence stretched out too long.

"Oh, same old, same old. Trying to convince Mom and Dad to take a vacation to somewhere warm while it's the slow season." Louisa took Anna's normal seat—which happened to be right next to Palmer's.

Grant entered the kitchen after a few moments, dropping a kiss on his girlfriend's cheek before taking his seat at the table. It wasn't really all that strange to see Dahlia at their table now. She seemed to fit right in with the flow of things, and Grant had certainly been less sour and uptight since Dahlia had come around.

Who could blame him? Dahlia was a looker, and a sweetheart to boot. She'd taken a job at the local library and seemed to fit right in there too.

It was a normal dinner. The kind they'd had a million times before. Louisa could be part of the family for as many meals as she'd eaten with them over the years. Of course, usually Anna was there, but Louisa was friends with everyone.

She might have a smart mouth, but that just made for a good fit at the Hudson table. She also knew how to make people laugh, particularly Cash's eleven-year-old. It was hard to imagine her at the O'Brien orchard with just her parents, who were considerably older than she was.

Considerably older. She was an only child. Could it really be possible she was some kidnapped baby? The O'Briens were…kind, quiet people. Oh, Tim O'Brien could talk your ear off about apple varieties and grafting, and Minnie was a member of every county quilting, baking and charity group that appeared at the whiff of tragedy, but they were just…normal.

Surely this was just… Well, he couldn't believe Louisa had been taken in by a scam. She was whip-smart and almost as cynical as his sister. But underneath that sardonic shell, she had a softer heart than Anna. Maybe she was simply entertaining this whole thing because she felt badly for the girl who'd lost her sister.

He studied her, trying to work out the angles of the story she'd told him outside. She was just missing something. He'd help her figure it out tonight and then that would be it.

Twenty-four hours tops.

Her gaze shifted to his and almost immediately darted away—until she realized he'd been staring at her. Then she turned her head and gave him a questioning look.

It really wasn't fair. If she'd been any random woman in any random bar, that green gaze would lead to a fun night or two and that would be it. It wouldn't tangle inside him, all barbs and strange feelings.

Because she was mixed up with his family in deep, thorny ways that couldn't be dug out of, she felt different. It wasn't *her*. It was the situation.

So, he'd fix the situation and get her on her way.

They ate, they chatted. Mary brought out dessert while Cash and Jack argued over whose turn it was to do dishes. Palmer didn't bother to add to the argument, though it was a grand tradition that dated back to childhood.

Mary kept the schedule, knew who did what and when, and never failed to swoop in and tell them what was what. It was why she always handled the meals. Her ultraorganized brain couldn't stand the rest of them messing up her very careful processes.

Jack's phone buzzed as they all lingered over dessert. Since he was the sheriff of Sunrise, he—and he alone—was allowed to keep his phone at the table during the family meal.

Not that Palmer didn't *occasionally* check his

or make his evening plans under the table when no one was looking.

"Storm blew in a bit sooner than we anticipated," Jack said, reading his text. "Deputy Brink says roads are already a mess." Jack looked up at those who didn't live at the main Hudson house. "Everyone might want to think about bunking here tonight."

Izzy let out a little whoop of celebration, causing Cash to frown and the dogs to begin barking and yipping themselves. Dahlia and Grant just made moony eyes over each other. And…well, Palmer didn't dare look at Louisa.

As Jack began to clear the table—because it *was* his turn—Cash ushered Izzy out of the room with threats of homework and a bath, and Mary disappeared so as not to nitpick the cleaning-up process. Dahlia and Grant offered some lame excuse about going to *read*, and before Palmer could make a quip like, "So, that's what the kids are calling it these days," Louisa leaned over.

"Don't worry," she whispered, patting his arm. "I'll sneak into your room later."

Palmer sat stock-still.

Well. Now he *was* worried.

LOUISA HAD BEEN spending nights at the Hudson house since she was a little girl. She'd always stayed in Anna's room, whether they'd been kids or grown women. It felt natural to take Anna's room now, even with her not there.

The Hudsons had always made her feel welcome—before and after their parents' disappearance. She'd never once felt uncomfortable in this house. Even now, as she crept down the hall to Palmer's room, dressed in Anna's pajamas that she'd borrowed, *comfortable*.

Well, until Mary popped up on the stairs, causing Louisa to jump a foot and let out a little shriek of surprise.

Mary laughed. "Oh, I'm sorry. I didn't mean to startle you."

"It's not your fault," Louisa replied, laughing too, because, honestly… "I just thought everyone was asleep."

Mary looked from where Louisa had come to where she was *clearly* going. She blinked. Once. "You're not…" Mary trailed off. She was only two years older than Louisa and Anna, but far more…introverted and contained. Still, she had played with them as girls and sometimes hung out with them now as women—as long as they weren't going to bars or staying out late.

She also, more often than not, assumed the role of designated driver.

As much as Louisa considered Mary a friend, she wasn't her *best* friend, and she'd definitely never confided in Mary about her crush on Palmer.

"It's a prank," Louisa offered with a grin, lowering her voice into almost a whisper. "Promise."

Mary's relief seemed a bit *extreme* to Louisa's way of thinking. Would it really be *so* crazy if she was sneaking down the hall to twist the sheets with Palmer?

Do not let your imagination go down that lane of thought right now.

"Well, I am going to bed now, but if you need anything, just let me know."

"I know where everything is, Mary. Don't worry about me." She smiled at her friend and waited right where she was until Mary disappeared down the hall and into her own room.

Even after the door closed, Louisa waited a good two minutes before moving forward again. She wanted her wits about her when she dealt with Palmer. In his room. Late at night.

About helping you with your very serious issue, remember?

Right. Serious. Possible kidnapping and her parents were secretly evil somehow, when they'd always been loving and wonderful and *there.* And, okay, overindulgent to an extent, but Louisa thought she'd turned out fine despite it. Maybe she didn't *love* taking no for an answer, but who did? Maybe she *preferred* getting what she wanted, when she wanted it, but didn't everyone?

She wasn't afraid of hard work or patience or doing the hard things.

That was why she needed to stop procrastinating and go into Palmer's room to discuss her potential life-altering secrets.

She didn't bother to knock. If she secretly hoped she might catch a glimpse of Palmer partially disrobed... Well, no one needed to know that but her.

He was not, of course. He stood—fully clothed—staring out the window in his bedroom at the dark, howling night. When she slid inside the room, he looked at her with a scowl.

"Not even a knock?"

Louisa didn't bother to acknowledge that comment. She studied the room around her. She'd been in his room before. Usually for the kind of pranks two little girls liked to play on an older brother. Palmer had always been Anna's favorite target, probably because instead of getting mad or trying to pull older-brother rank in a house without parents, Palmer just retaliated.

Things *had* changed since then. He no longer had posters of scantily clad women and bull riders and cars all over his room. Football gear and ranch wear wasn't littered over every surface. This was no longer a boy's room. At some point, it had turned into a man's.

Sure, a little messy—some dirty clothes littered here and there, way too many cowboy hats on way too many surfaces and a decidedly unmade bed—but it was mostly solid colors and sparse decorations.

It was oddly sad in a way. That he'd gone from decorating his rooms with all his interests to hiding it all behind…whatever this was.

And since she was sad and didn't want to dwell on it when her own life made her sad enough at the moment, she set out to irritate him.

"Mary thought I was off to drum up a booty call, I think." She plopped onto his bed, testing the bounce.

He stood—completely and utterly frozen—as far from the bed as he could get. She grinned at him, waiting for him to stop looking at her in horror.

Again, the *over*reaction irked—she wasn't exactly a child or a hideous beast—but she didn't let that show. She pulled her phone out of the pocket of the sweatpants she'd borrowed from Anna's closet.

"Let me show you a few things my maybe-sister sent me." She patted the spot next to her on the bed.

Palmer didn't move. She looked up at him, doing her level best to appear innocently confused. "What's the problem?"

"No problem," he said gruffly when he was almost never gruff. Stiffly, he moved over to the bed. Very carefully, he perched himself on the very edge of the mattress. Like he was afraid someone might burst in and accuse them of that booty call.

Heaven forbid.

She shook off her irritation—this wasn't the time or place. She'd tuck it away for later.

"First up is the picture of her." She held out her phone.

"There's a resemblance," Palmer said after a while.

"We're practically twins."

"That happens. I don't think it's a reason to believe your parents might be monsters. Even your parents' overreaction to the DNA test thing is understandable. Those companies have your DNA. There's a lot of questionable practices. You're working with a lot of circumstantial evidence and making a *giant* leap."

As if she didn't know that? Hadn't struggled with it for *months*? "Okay, so how can we work with facts that prove something? Do you think I *want* to be some poor kidnapped baby?"

"Well, no. But—"

"No buts. I hate this. I don't want it. There are just too many questions for me to ignore. And I... I don't know what to do next." It was hard to admit that to anyone, let alone Palmer. She didn't deal in uncertainty. She and Anna had that in common. They charged ahead, damn the consequences. These consequences were just too big. "I don't know how to...move forward."

"I suppose asking them is out of the question."

She sent him a scathing glare. She could just imagine the look on her mother's face. The utter hurt and devastation. The way it would change their family *forever*. Because her parents would always know she'd doubted them when they'd never given her reason to.

And if this whole insane story were true? "I need proof, Palmer."

He sighed and raked a hand through his hair. "Okay. Give me the family's names. I'll see what I can dig up."

Chapter Three

Louisa threw her arms around Palmer's neck. Right there on his bed.

"Thank you," she said, squeezing him to her. "I knew you wouldn't let me down."

It shouldn't have surprised him. Louisa was very…physical. Where Anna liked to kick and punch her way out of a situation, her best friend had always been about big hugs and linking arms and bumping hips and giving impromptu squeezes.

But, you know, never on his *bed*.

Palmer closed his eyes and thought of taxes. Calculators. The noise the dogs made when they ate too fast.

Anything but the way she felt with her arms around him. On his *bed*—

He pulled her arms off him. He didn't *jump* from the bed, because Louisa was too smart and too mean not to give him a hard time for that. But he eased off the mattress and frowned down at her.

"The names, Louisa?"

"Right." She looked down at the phone in her hand. "I'll text them to you." She tapped on her phone screen a few times and his phone on the nightstand chimed a few seconds later.

"I really do appreciate your help and…" She chewed on her bottom lip as she stood. A distracting habit he knew better than to focus on. Or had known better, before she'd entered his room. "I know you… It's just…"

"Spit it out, Lou."

She sighed, not reacting to the snap in his tone. "Please don't tell anyone. Not Anna, not your brothers. No one. I have to proceed with this believing it's a fool's errand. If anyone but you knew about me even looking into it, I would be too embarrassed to show my face anywhere."

"I'm not going to tell anyone," he muttered. Didn't that go without saying?

She didn't hug him this time, but she did reach out and squeeze his arm. Her green eyes were uncharacteristically soft. "Thank you, Palmer."

He only grunted—which reminded him way too much of his eldest brother. Palmer might have all the love and respect for Jack in the world, but he'd made every choice *ever* not to follow in his brother's uptight, stuck-in-the-mud, martyred footsteps.

Louisa slipped out of his room and he took his first full breath of the evening, but it still smelled too much like her. Vanilla and the hint of earth that seemed ever a part of her, like growing up on that orchard had made her one with the trees.

He shook *that* fanciful thought out of his head and eyed his bed. No. Bad idea.

So even though it was late, he did not go to sleep. He was terrified of what might visit him in dreams if he did. He went down to the room they'd converted into a kind of security office, where he kept his computers. He looked at his phone and the names Louisa had texted him and got to it.

Like most computer work, he started with the easy. The surface stuff. Basic records anyone could see, news articles about the baby's disappearance. Then, once he'd exhausted that, he started to dig deeper. Past where your average Joe would know to or how to look.

Everything appeared normal. Louisa O'Brien existed in a completely separate life from Kyla Brown and her family in Lakely, Ohio. There was no connection, no overlap between the Browns and the O'Briens. Palmer couldn't find evidence the Browns had ever been to Wyoming or that the O'Briens had ever been to Ohio. There wasn't even any visible and plausible reason the Browns would want to trick Louisa into believing this scheme. They'd divorced almost fifteen years ago, and both their separate finances seemed to be in decent order. Mr. Brown had a little bit of a rap sheet for battery, and Palmer would keep digging into that, but he couldn't see how that would connect to the daughter reaching out to Louisa.

All of what he found should have proved exactly what Louisa wanted: the idea she was the missing baby was absurd and impossible.

But…

A little hack into hospital records did not yield the results Palmer had hoped for. He couldn't track down Mrs. O'Brien's hospital records for Louisa's birth, though he could find other hospital records for all the O'Briens at different points in their lives.

It wasn't proof of anything, one way or another. But it raised a question—when he'd wanted irrefutable evidence that raised *no* questions and would get Louisa as far out of his hair as his baby sister's best friend could get.

A little while later when his alarm went off, he hadn't slept a wink, and didn't have any clear-cut way to prove to Louisa she should let this go. So, when he stepped out into the wild white of the Hudson Ranch the night after a blizzard, his usual jovial attitude was nowhere to be found.

It was good though, to trudge through the snow. To have to physically exert himself enough his brain wasn't full of Louisa. He made it to the barn and found that Cash was already there. Palmer moved forward and helped his brother dig the barn door out of the snow enough to get it open.

"Quite a storm," Cash commented by way of greeting. "We're going to need to do perimeter checks. Jack and Grant already dug out the shed and got those snowmobiles. They're driving down to pick up the ranch hands," Cash explained, referring to the small ranch staff they kept on year-round. They bunked down on the south side of the ranch. "They'll split up and handle the back portion. Mary's on Izzy duty, so it's just you and me up here. Best go in pairs."

Palmer nodded as he followed Cash deeper into the barn toward the remainder of the snowmobiles they kept always ready to go during the winter. The horses puffed in greeting. Mary and Izzy would come out and feed and water them once it got a little warmer, because even in blizzards the Hudsons all had roles and knew them.

"Hey, guys," a feminine voice greeted. Both he and Cash turned to Louisa standing in the entrance to the barn. She was wearing Anna's ranch gear, but there was no mistaking her for Anna.

"What are you doing?" Palmer demanded as she approached.

"It's a lot of work digging out of this," Louisa said, looking fresher than anyone had a right to in the midst of all this blinding white. "I'm here to help."

"We could use it," Cash said before Palmer had the chance to tell her to turn right back around and leave him the hell alone.

That would have been an overreaction, all things considered, but he still wanted to indulge.

"Palmer and I will get the snowmobiles out. Can you go let Marsh out of his pen?" Cash said, referring to one of the dogs that spent its nights in the dog pens in the barn with the horses. There weren't a lot of places on the ranch that didn't bunk Cash's huge canine menagerie overnight. "I'll take him with me, then you and Palmer can go together. Split our section. We'll get everything done quicker."

"Sure," Louisa agreed cheerfully, then turned and disappeared into the far section of the barn.

Palmer didn't realize he was glaring after her until Cash nudged him.

"Even you're not foolish enough to go there," Cash said on a half whisper.

Palmer didn't let himself immediately react. If he had anything going for him, even with his temper on boil, it was that he was not a man prone to behaving rashly. When he made bad decisions, he liked to spend some time relishing them.

He turned his head to look at his brother slowly. Maybe not calmly, but not reactively. There was a teasing glint in Cash's eyes, but there was something in the expression that spoke of *actual* worry. Nothing could have set Palmer's teeth on edge more.

"Go where?" Palmer said, letting the edge in his voice ring loud and clear.

Cash rolled his eyes. "You're practically drooling. Over *Louisa*. And I get it, but I'm reminding you to think with your brain instead of your favorite appendage." He got on his snowmobile and Palmer executed the same movement in unison on his.

"I… What do you mean? You *get* it?"

Cash gestured toward where Louisa had disappeared. "She's pretty. But she practically grew up here and is Anna's best friend. Growing up pretty isn't an excuse for you to be yourself. You hear me?"

"What I hear is you trying to play daddy—and I'm not sure if it's to me or to Louisa, but neither of us need it."

"What *I* hear is you very much not denying things you should be denying."

Palmer shot Cash a look. He knew he should smile and laugh it off, but that his brother thought so little of him rankled. "Because you're my judge and jury?"

"No, but Jack will be, and Anna will run right home to play executioner." Cash turned on his snowmobile and idled it outside. Palmer had no choice but to follow. When they were both stopped outside, Palmer killed his engine and leaned toward his brother.

"Maybe it's none of y'all's business, Cash."

Cash laughed. Actually laughed. "Since when did that matter around here?" He sobered quickly. "You cannot mess around with Louisa O'Brien. It shouldn't even need to be said."

Palmer knew what his response should be. He knew how to handle this. Maybe he'd blame it on the lack of sleep, or the fact that he was actually helping Louisa, that he did none of the things he *should*.

He grinned at his brother, hunching deeper into the warmth of his coat. "Guess we'll see." Then he marched back into the barn. Marsh came bounding around the corner and Palmer paused to crouch and give the dog a good pet. "Do me a favor, Marsh," he muttered to the dog, "bite him. Right in the ass."

Marsh bounded outside to Cash like he was going to obey the order, but Palmer knew he wouldn't, considering Cash did all the dog training around here.

Palmer straightened as Louisa walked around the corner. The heavy winter clothes hid her figure, her hair, everything that made her *her*.

Except her eyes and her mouth and the freckles on her nose and—damn it all to hell. "Come on," he muttered, taking her elbow and all but dragging her outside.

Cash took off, Marsh sitting happily in the little snowmobile addition Cash had jerry-rigged for the dogs. Palmer hesitated as they approached his. In a storm like this, it was best to go in pairs on one machine. Check the fences and the cattle. Make sure no one got lost or hurt or too cold.

But he didn't want her pressed up against him in *any* capacity. He should convince her to go back inside. He kept walking toward his machine and all he could think of was what Cash had said. What Louisa said Mary had thought last night.

"What is it with my siblings thinking I'm out to seduce you?" he demanded.

She shrugged, though he couldn't help but notice a small hitch in her stride when he'd said *seduce*. "You seduce everything."

"Not *you*," he gritted out. Gritted because he was working very hard not to picture *that*.

They stopped at the snowmobile and she turned to face him. "If you haven't noticed, Palmer, I look good. Everyone in Sunrise knows you like things that look good."

It was true and yet, when *she* said it, it did nothing but tick him off. And create something wholly twisted and unwelcome deep in his gut. "I know what people think of me. Hell, I know what *I* think of me. But there are rules even *I* have always followed. No married women. No messing around with my sister's *friends*."

"Wasn't Mary friends with Freya? You messed around with her. And what about your brothers' female friends. Are *they* okay to 'mess around' with?"

He opened his mouth to argue with her but found no words.

"The whole thing is kind of archaic, don't you think?"

He pressed his gloved fingers to his temples. "I think I don't know how we got on this topic of conversation."

She opened her mouth, but he shook his head.

"That was *not* an invitation to explain how." He sighed heavily then straddled the snowmobile. He needed cold air and hard work and none of *this* conversation. When she didn't immediately climb on behind him, he glared over at her. "Are you getting on?"

She blinked as she looked from the seat to his face. "Yeah. *Duh.*" But there was something… strange about how she held herself. For someone who'd hugged him with absolutely no tension *in his bed* last night, she climbed on gingerly, like she'd never ridden a snowmobile in her life.

When she'd once created an incredibly dangerous course with Anna, and he'd watched her do ill-advised jumps into the air with one.

Jack had read them all the riot act.

It had been worth it.

This time around, they were adults, and she slid onto the seat behind him. They were separated by layers and layers of clothes meant to keep the cold Wyoming winter at bay. Even her arms wrapped around his middle as he took off into the snowy pastures were heavily padded.

This was nothing. They weren't really pressed together at all. He thought about the tuna casserole his grandma used to make that he hated, dive bar bathrooms, that time his friend's tobacco spit cup had upended all over his truck.

They puttered along the fence line, looking for damaged fencing or cattle that might look to be in distress. Palmer stopped at one place where the barbed wire drooped. Without him having to say a word, Louisa grabbed the tool bag from the compartment on the side of the snowmobile.

They worked in complete silence, using pliers and wire cutters to repair the fence. The sun had come out and Palmer gave half a thought to ditching his outermost layer, but he'd no doubt regret it on the ride back.

Back home. Where they'd be surrounded by people. So, he might as well discuss what little he'd found. "I did some digging last night," he said. "Not one overlap between your family and the Browns."

"Last night? What did you do? Stay up all night?"

Palmer shrugged. "You want this over, don't you?"

"Yes, I do. But I don't want you to… I need your help, but if I'd wanted someone to martyr themselves to my cause, I would have gone to Jack."

Another truth that rankled, deep and sharp. "Why don't you?"

She was quiet as they finished tying off the wire. He handed her the tools and she put them away as he gave the wire a testing pull. "Good," he muttered. He moved for the snowmobile, but she stepped in his way, putting her hand on his chest.

Gloved hand. Many layers of clothes on his chest. And yet…

Hell, he needed to find those hospital records so this could be over.

"You don't have to help me if you don't want to, Palmer," she said. Her voice, so firm and devoid of any blame, reminded him of an elementary school teacher.

Putting him firmly in his place.

"I want to help. I just don't want my methods questioned."

"Fair enough," she said in that same obnoxious tone. "Did you find anything that proves I *am* my parents' child?"

He wanted to lie to her, but he couldn't. It wouldn't be right and…he just couldn't. "Not yet. I'm trying to find hospital records of your birth."

"Trying?"

"Yeah." He could see the wheels in her head turning. "But not everything is computerized, even for someone as young as you. So, it's not proof of anything. Okay?"

Louisa did not panic. Well, internally she was panicking, but she didn't let it come out. She just stood very still and kept her gaze on Palmer.

He was steady. A Hudson rock. The brothers might be different, but they looked mostly alike.

Like their father before them. Tall and broad, dark-haired and charming smiles—though Palmer was the freest with his.

Louisa had spent far too much time as a teenager looking at *Palmer's* dark eyes when he smiled, determining what each different angle and width of smile really meant.

He wasn't smiling now, and she had no idea what anything meant. He said it wasn't proof.

"There should obviously be a hospital record," she managed to say, focusing on the darker ring of brown along the edges of his irises.

"Sure, but there's a lot of reasons why they might not be where I looked. Or maybe your mom gave birth somewhere else. Maybe she had a home birth?"

Louisa shook her head. "I mean, I know I don't remember since I was all of a day old, but they always talk about bringing me home from the hospital."

"Okay. Maybe once the roads clear up and you go home, you can find a way to ask. Or even poke around files or something. It isn't proof until we can prove there's *no* record."

"But…"

"Lou." He said her shortened named gently, and he took her arm and gave it a squeeze. "Don't jump to conclusions. Not yet."

She swallowed and nodded. "Of course not."

The sensible thing was to focus on all the plausible reasons he couldn't find a hospital record for her. Too bad her heart felt like it was being twisted in a vise. She'd poked through her parents' files. She didn't recall seeing any kind of hospital record, just her birth certificate.

She hadn't been looking for that, had she? She hadn't really known *what* she'd been looking for. And she'd been so afraid…

She cleared her throat and tried to focus on the task at hand. "We should finish our section."

He didn't move. He didn't let go of her arm. And the expression on his face was somehow… not pity. Why should it be? His parents had disappeared without a trace and no one had figured out what happened to them.

Even if she hated what she learned, it would be clear. It would be…terrible, yes, but not as traumatizing as losing your parents at twelve and never knowing *why*.

She was rooted to the spot, to his eyes, to the knowledge there was no hospital record of her birth.

"Louisa, we'll get answers. I promise you that. Even if they're not the ones you want, you're going to be okay."

She nodded, but she did not move. He muttered a curse then pulled her to him. She tried to think of it as a sort of big-brother gesture.

She knew that's what he thought of her. Anna's friend. Another little pest.

Even if he *had* said the word *seduce* in her presence and it had made her desperately want to know what that was like.

To Palmer Hudson, she would always be a little girl.

He gave her a nice hug and patted her back and said reassuring words about getting to the bottom of things.

"I promise," he even murmured in her ear.

That, he couldn't actually *promise*. He didn't know there were answers to find. Sometimes, you didn't find out anything—as he well knew.

But she felt comforted anyway.

Chapter Four

The more time Palmer spent digging into Louisa's actual birth records, the more frustrated he became. Computers had always been a natural thing for him. He liked to tinker. He liked to laser focus into one problem and had no trouble failing time and time again without getting frustrated.

It was a bit like climbing on the back of a bull or a bucking bronc. If you just kept trying, eventually things worked out. And with computers, you were less likely to break your skull.

More likely to get arrested though, if you hacked into the wrong program.

They had to find you first. So he'd searched and hacked and searched some more, and there was still no authentic record of Louisa's actual birth. Checkups ever since, but no birth hospital record.

There could be a very reasonable explanation for that. Everything about the O'Briens was normal. Run-of-the-mill. There weren't even any major financial transactions—either way—in the period around Louisa's birth. No trips. Nothing odd.

Yet this one thing didn't add up. The fact that it didn't dug under Palmer's skin like a burr, making him uncharacteristically grumpy and short, to the point *Jack* of all people pointed it out.

"What crawled up your butt and died?"

Palmer studied his older brother, all decked out in his sheriff's uniform—which was just jeans and a button-up and that damn star badge he was so proud of—over the breakfast table. They had both already been out in the howling cold this morning and were now lingering at the breakfast table over coffee.

"Maybe whatever crawled up yours found a new home," Palmer returned, flashing a grin at his brother.

Before Jack could respond, Palmer's phone vibrated in his pocket and he pulled it out rather than deal with Jack.

It was a text from Louisa.

Can you come to the orchard sometime this afternoon? Mom and Dad are going to be gone from 1-3, and I want some help snooping.

He frowned at his phone.

Why can't you do it yourself?

She sent him an eye roll emoji, followed by a block of text that made him roll his actual eyes.

What do you think I've been doing for the past few days? I need fresh eyes and maybe someone who's sneakier about hiding things like you used to hide your beer in the hayloft behind the loose board in the northwest corner.

He smiled a little at that. He'd always known someone had found his stash. He'd always suspected Cash and his high school girlfriend—now ex-wife—but Anna and Louisa made just about as much sense.

I always knew you two were thieving—

"Who are you texting?"

Palmer jumped about a foot. Not because the question startled him so much as *who* was asking. He glared up at Anna. "Hell in a handbasket. When did you decide to grace us with your presence?"

"Once the job was done," she returned, still trying to see who he was texting even though he'd moved his phone completely under the table. "Who are you texting?" she asked again. "With that dopey grin on your face."

"You always think my face looks dopey."

"This was *especially* dopey."

Without taking his gaze from Anna, he held down the button so his phone shut off. "Just planning on meeting someone at the Lariat tonight."

"Someone special?"

Jack snorted from the other end of the table. "Special? He probably doesn't even know her name."

Palmer forced himself to grin, though in his mind's eye he was punching Jack square in the nose. "If love can be blind, love can be nameless," he drawled, pushing back from the table.

As he'd known she would, Anna swiped the phone out of his hand when he tried to move past her. Hence why he'd turned it off.

She scowled at the blank screen then lifted her gaze to glare at him. "I know your passcode."

"No, you don't."

She huffed, a clear sign she was bluffing. "I could figure it out."

"Not before I got it back, you couldn't. Now, do you mind? I got things to do."

"What things?" Jack demanded, still sitting and drinking his coffee at the head of the table. Palmer always thought Jack resembled their father—more with every passing year—but it was in the mornings, with the Christmas lights twinkling and him sitting in Dad's chair, that it struck through Palmer like a pain.

"I'll send you an itinerary, drill sergeant," he said gruffly. Then, since Anna was distracted by looking at Jack, Palmer plucked his phone back and headed out of the dining room. He turned his phone back on and inwardly groaned at the *ten* text messages.

No doubt all from Louisa.

He took a quick glance behind him to see if Anna had followed him to the front of the house. She hadn't. Yet.

He grabbed his cowboy hat, settled it on his head and shrugged into his coat. It was still a cold, windy mess out there, but the roads had been cleared. So that the ranch looked like a Christmas postcard.

Palmer braced himself against the chill and headed for his truck. He kept expecting Anna to jump out at him and hurl more demanding questions, but she didn't.

And that, in and of itself, was suspicious.

Once safely in his truck, he looked at the texts Louisa had sent. Mostly chastising about his lack of response.

I'm saving you from Anna getting involved. You're welcome.

Are you coming or not?

On my way.

He tossed the cell into the passenger seat then started driving for the O'Brien apple orchard. He didn't have any compunction about snooping around the O'Brien house. That wasn't the cause of the churning weight in his gut. The way he saw it, he was doing them a favor.

If they *hadn't* stolen Louisa, and hell it was hard to believe they *had*, then he was saving them the emotional turmoil of *all that*. If they had? Well. They deserved what they got.

What concerned him was being in a house all alone with Louisa. *Not* because anything was going to happen, just because the woman was…

Okay, he could admit it in the privacy of his own head. She was terrifying. Stubborn and funny and comfortable in her own skin. And, worst of all, emotionally vulnerable. He didn't want to touch *that* with a million-foot pole.

Still, he took the turn to the orchard that would fork eventually and lead him to the house. He supposed it didn't matter if people saw him driving to the O'Briens'. He was friendly with all of them, and he could make up any number of reasons for his truck to be seen driving down the gravel drive.

But he had a bad feeling he and Louisa needed to be careful so the town gossips didn't start *wondering*.

They wouldn't know what they were *really* doing, but the potential of what they *could* be doing would spread through town like wild-fire. Get to his brothers and, worse, Anna, in record time.

And what would he say? He couldn't very well tell anyone the truth any more than he could play along with potential gossip that he and Louisa were…involved.

No, no one would say *involved*. They would think, given it was him, it had to be a hookup. Sunrise residents might very well throw him in a cattle car and hope he ended up in the Ne-braska prairie like the history lore said his an-cestors did when a dangerous element tried to take over the town.

The house came into view. It was already decorated for Christmas—it was daylight, so no lights shone, but he could see the bright col-ors of the bulbs anyway. Wooden Santas and snowmen he knew Tim had made himself and Minnie had painted.

Louisa was waiting for him on the porch. Her nose was red, so she'd been outside for a little bit. He ignored the kick in his gut by getting out of the truck with a lecture on his lips.

"What are you doing? Trying to catch your death of cold?"

"What are you doing?" she retorted. "Trying to do an imitation of my mother?"

He frowned at her as he climbed the stairs of the porch, stomping the snow off his boots.

She looked up at him, and even though she'd had a snarky response, he could see all the worry, guilt and anxiety in her eyes. "Dad's at a doctor's appointment, and he always ends up chatting with Dr. Phillips then heading over to the Coffee Klatsch to gossip with whoever else is up there. Mom's at a church meeting until three, but she'll likely stay after checking on the Christmas poinsettias and who knows what else." She wrung her hands together, squinted at the drive toward the highway, then shot a guilty glance at the house. "Let's get this over with."

"You really don't have to—"

She held up a hand and waved it as she opened the front door. "Don't tell me I don't have to because I *do* have to. I need answers. And you haven't been able to prove to me that I should stop looking."

No, he hadn't. Since that ate at him, he didn't say anything as she led him through the house. He hadn't been in here much. The O'Briens hosted town events sometimes at the orchard, so he'd spent plenty of summer afternoons and evenings out among the apple trees, but he'd only stepped foot inside the actual house once or twice.

It was a lot like Hudson Ranch, except everything was on a smaller scale and seemed a little…older. Where he was certain, at home, Mary didn't let a single board or windowsill dare splinter, wilt or warp.

"All the paperwork for us, for the orchard, Dad keeps in his office. I've searched everything in there and found nothing. I've poked through their room a little, but no luck. And before you say, *Maybe there's nothing to be found*, let's skip the argument. Look around a bit, and if you can't find anything in an hour, we'll give it up."

Since she seemed *this* close to breaking, he didn't offer any advice or alternatives. He just nodded once. "Okay. Show me the files."

Louisa wasn't sure which annoyed her more—when Palmer argued with her or when he *didn't*. Because when he didn't, she knew he felt sorry for her. She *hated* that.

Of course, she hated all of this, and she just knew…there had to be something. Something here.

Palmer took a seat at her father's desk and meticulously pulled every drawer open. He looked through files and every single paper. He was thorough.

Just when she was sure he was going to look up at her and tell her there was nothing to be found, that she should give up and leave him alone, he pointed to the little corner cubby of the desk.

"Do you have the key to this?"

"Key to what?"

Palmer pointed again, but she didn't see a keyhole. It was just a little decorative cubby. At least, that's what she'd always thought. Until Palmer reached out and pulled back a section of the wood—almost like a door, although she couldn't make out a hinge. And there in the exposed wood *was* a keyhole.

Louisa's vision threatened to gray, but she took a breath. It was just a small compartment in the corner of the desk. Sure, it was a secret compartment, but it was an old desk. Maybe there was nothing in there. She cleared her throat before she trusted herself to speak. "I don't know where a key that small would be."

Palmer shrugged. "No worries." He took his wallet from his back pocket and opened it on the desk surface. There was a little collection of bills, a condom, which she desperately tried not to think about, and a little bobby pin, which he pulled out.

"Have a lot of hair emergencies?" she asked acidly, because it looked like a memento and something about the sentimentality of it was worse than the practicality of a condom in his wallet.

He just grinned at her then pushed the bobby pin into the small keyhole. He fiddled with it for a while, until the door popped open. When she didn't move, didn't say anything, he looked at her.

Really looked at her. In that way he had that no one else did. Everyone thought they knew her. Parents. Teachers. Friends. Even Anna thought she knew everything there was to know about Louisa.

No one had predicted she'd want to go to Massachusetts for college though. No one had expected her to throw herself into a collegiate softball career then quit. Wholesale. And when she did things like that, everyone just thought it was a one off.

But Palmer had always looked. Tried to make sense of it. Because he was the same. Everyone thought they knew him, the carefree football star and rodeo cowboy who hadn't been as marked by his parents' disappearance as his siblings.

When he had been. Of course he had been.

"Lou?"

She swallowed, trying to shake herself out of her reverie. Better to think of Palmer and all he was than what might be hidden in that compartment.

Because he was staring at her, trying to see

who she was in this moment, she told him the truth. "I don't think I can look at whatever is in there."

Something in his expression softened and she wasn't sure she wanted anything to do with Palmer's softness, but fear of what was inside that compartment overrode everything else.

"We're here because you want answers. If you wanted easy, or to do things without being afraid, we wouldn't be here. So, you might not want to look, but you're certainly capable of looking."

She knew she was capable. The point was she didn't *want* to be. She didn't want to face something that could potentially change her life forever. Why else would her father have a secret desk compartment?

"I'm right here," Palmer said, standing. He put his hand on her shoulder, both reassurance and a gentle nudge to take a seat in the desk chair. "No matter what you find. You know you've got friends, Lou. We'll get you through."

She sucked in a breath.

"Go on now."

Usually people telling her what to do was an irritation. Usually Palmer telling her what to do was more challenge than anything else. But in this moment, it helped. She reached forward and—

From nowhere, Palmer's hand flew out and stopped her forward movement. Without a word, he shut the little compartment's door and eased the wood slat that covered it back into place.

By then, Louisa heard why. Footsteps. She sucked in a breath and held it. How was she going to explain…?

A man appeared in the doorway. Not either of her parents. Louisa jumped out of her chair and she might have toppled over if Palmer hadn't been there to gently keep her upright.

"Grandpa," she squeaked in greeting. "What are you doing here?"

Chapter Five

Palmer had often been caught red-handed. Usually it involved dark rooms and fewer clothes. He didn't embarrass easily, because if he was doing something, he'd already decided not to be ashamed of it.

This was, of course, different. Still, Palmer didn't really react. That was usually the best defense. Louisa was all fifty shades of red, stuttering over her words with uncharacteristic fidgeting.

"Am I not allowed to visit my son's house? On the orchard my grandfather built from the ground up?" Greg O'Brien said, eyeing Palmer. Not Louisa.

That, Palmer figured, was a good thing in the short term. If Greg was suspicious of Palmer's motives, he wouldn't be wondering why they were poking around Tim's desk.

Louisa laughed. It sounded deranged at best. "I'm just surprised to see you."

Greg's hard gaze never left Palmer. "Clearly."

"Uh." Louisa blinked up at him like she was surprised to still find him there. "Palmer was just..."

Palmer decided there was only one way out of this. He didn't like it. Hated it in fact. But it kept suspicion at bay, and he knew that's what Louisa wanted more than anything. So he grinned at Greg. "Lou here needed a lightbulb changed."

Greg's expression went thunderous, and poor Louisa—who wasn't all that naive but clearly new to subterfuge—just looked confused at what a poor excuse that was.

"That so," Greg said between gritted teeth.

"Yes, sir," Palmer replied, not letting his smile dim in the least. "But it's all changed now, so I can be on my way. I'll see you later, Lou." He grabbed his hat and slid it on his head, making sure it looked to Greg like he was giving Louisa a long *lingering* look when what he was really doing was making sure the secret compartment was all covered up.

Palmer didn't wait for Louisa to respond. He sauntered on past her grandfather and into the living room. He took his sweet time—no hurrying. He knew how to look like a man who'd just enjoyed himself.

Thoroughly.

Lord, he hoped Greg O'Brien wasn't half the

gossip his wife was. Of course, one stray word to Louisa's grandmother and Palmer would find himself with Anna holding a knife to his throat by dinner.

Metaphorically.

Probably.

Palmer took the stairs. Usually the orchard was a pretty sight, but something about looking out at all those bare trees in the snow had a creeping sensation crawling up his spine. Like someone was out there. Watching.

That was absurd because there was nowhere to hide with leafless branches and only the slight rolling hills that separated one apple variety from another.

He glanced back at the house, all cheerful-Christmas decorated, but it didn't settle that odd *off* feeling inside him. He'd learned long ago that those feelings didn't really matter. Everything felt wrong when your parents disappeared without a trace. Everything felt wrong when you threw yourself into getting hit as hard as possible—by football opponents, by charging bulls, by angry men in seedy bars.

Wrong became normal. Accepting it, one of those life lessons. Still, he couldn't quite make himself move and leave Louisa alone.

She isn't alone. She's with her grandfather.

Who, speak of the devil, stepped out onto

the porch before Palmer'd had the good sense to leave.

Greg O'Brien didn't look to be leaving, but he did look to be handing out lectures. Palmer sighed and waited.

"My granddaughter isn't one of your bar floozies," the man said. Low and clear. There were no threats, but he didn't need to offer one. The commentary was enough.

Palmer didn't respond right away. He also didn't back down from Greg O'Brien's angry gaze. He held it. Cool. Though his own temper stirred, he didn't let it out. He took his sweet time sliding his hands into his pockets and pretending to consider Greg's words.

"I appreciate the concern, Mr. O'Brien, but I don't consider anyone a *floozy*. It's an outdated term, don't you think? After all, how a woman chooses to spend her time—and who with—is kind of her business, isn't it?"

"Now, listen here—"

Palmer had no patience to *listen*. Or to be lectured for something he hadn't even done. He lectured himself plenty just for *thinking* about it.

"I'm sure Louisa can decide who she wants to spend her time with all on her own," Palmer continued with as little inflection on any of those words as possible. Then he calmly turned around and crunched through the snow back to his truck.

All the while, Greg sputtered.

When Palmer got in his pickup and drove down the lane, that uneasy feeling followed. He tried to ignore it, push it away, but it was persistent. When he looked in the rearview mirror at the O'Brien house…all he could think about was all those *what-ifs* he'd trained himself not to think about when it came to *literally* everyone else.

Apparently, when it came to Louisa, he was sunk.

Louisa didn't know quite how to handle her grandfather. He was angry, and he did, on occasion, lose his temper, unlike his son, her father. But he was angry about all the wrong things, so she didn't know how to deal.

"Why don't I make you your afternoon coffee?" she offered. A distraction, hopefully. And they could get out of her father's office. Maybe he wouldn't think to mention it to her father.

Grandpa grunted then turned on a heel and left the room. She gave one last look around the office, making sure it was as it was when she and Palmer had come in, then scurried after him.

He wasn't in the kitchen. He was standing

outside on the porch, and she could see through the kitchen window that Palmer was standing there at the foot of the stairs, listening to whatever her grandfather had to say.

Palmer's jaw was tight and, when he spoke, she could see the frustration in his eyes. But whatever he said was delivered with a calmness she did not feel. Then he turned and strode to his truck.

When the front door slammed open, she wrenched her gaze from the window to her grandfather entering the kitchen.

She was not afraid of her grandfather, but he wasn't a warm man. Not like her father. There was a steely iron will to Greg O'Brien, and she'd never felt comfortable enough to butt heads with him.

Did it mean something?

"What are you staring at?" Grandpa demanded. "And what on earth are you doing with Palmer Hudson?"

She didn't want to answer either question, but she could hardly just stand in the kitchen gaping at him. "Palmer and I…are just friends," she said weakly.

He grunted. "I've never seen him sniffing around here before."

It had taken a few minutes, but she finally

had an explanation. "We're planning a surprise for Anna."

Grandpa only narrowed his eyes. "That boy is nothing but trouble."

She knew there was no reason to defend Palmer to her grandfather. People thought what they wanted to about Palmer, and it certainly wasn't up to her to stick up for him. Particularly when anyone she defended Palmer to would only consider her another hapless victim to his charms. "He's not a boy, and if he's getting into trouble, I suppose that's his choice."

Her grandfather's expression got all thunderous again.

"Is there something you came over for, Grandpa?" Louisa hurried on. "Dad and Mom are both in town. I was just about to organize some files for Dad when Palmer came over to deal with some things for Anna's surprise. Where's Grandma?"

"She's at that church meeting with your mother," he grumbled. He crossed over to her, doing something very out of character. He put his hand on her shoulder. "Louisa Jane. You're a good girl. You've got spirit and a good head on those shoulders, even if you did try to addle your brain out east. Trust me when I say Palmer Hudson is only going to lead to trouble."

It was hard to look past all these warnings

and lectures. She wasn't used to them from anyone. *She* didn't get lectures. Not really. Maybe some hopeful reminders, but not *lectures*.

Maybe that's why she could see beyond the irritation of this one to what was behind this whole strange thing.

Her grandfather was worried about her. And considering that small speech included the most compliments he'd ever leveled at her in her life, or maybe even *anyone* aside from John Wayne, she thought maybe it came from a good place. Even if he was wrong about Palmer and why Palmer had even been there.

So, she forced herself to smile. "Okay, Grandpa. Do you want that coffee?"

He agreed, and finally let the whole Palmer thing go.

When her parents got home, they didn't seem surprised to find him there with her. He stayed for dinner, which was kind of odd since he usually ate dinner with Grandma and, if the church meeting was over, she was likely at their house alone.

And he'd never explained why he'd come over.

Later, when she was washing dishes shoulder to shoulder with her mother while Dad was out with Grandpa puttering in the greenhouse, Louisa wasn't really paying attention to her mother.

She wasn't studying her in all the ways she had been these past few months, desperate to find similarities that were, in fact, skin deep.

She was thinking about the cubby in Dad's desk and if she hadn't been such a chicken they'd know what was in it. *Or you'd have been caught fully red-handed.*

Either way, how was she going to open it again? She didn't know how to pick locks like Palmer did, and she had some doubts about ever getting Palmer to come back out here after her grandfather's lecture.

She didn't think Palmer cared about lectures, per se, but she knew he hated the idea of anyone thinking he could possibly be in the least bit interested in her.

Which was really insulting. It wasn't that she needed him to be interested—obviously he wasn't and never would be. But he didn't have to be so *appalled* at the idea. He could admit that even if *he* didn't find her all that attractive, even if *he* always saw her as a child, she wasn't one. And didn't look like one.

"Louisa?"

Louisa blinked over at her mother, realizing by Mom's concerned stare that she really had been tuned out. "Sorry." She smiled. "Daydreaming. What did you say?"

Mom sighed but didn't press the issue because she was used to Louisa's flights of fancy, which, yes, far too often involved Palmer Hudson. "Did your grandfather say why he came out?" Mom asked.

"Oh. No." Did Mom think it was weird? *Was* it weird?

Mom got a thoughtful look on her face. "Huh."

"What?"

"It's just, your father and I both saw him in town. I mentioned your plans to go over to the Hudsons' this afternoon. So he knew the house was empty. It seems strange he'd come out here alone."

Louisa stared at her mother, her hands deep in the hot soapy water. "Why…would he do that?" she asked, trying not to sound as rattled as she felt.

"I suppose you were back in time to entertain him."

Which didn't actually answer Louisa's question.

And that was odd enough that it left Louisa feeling even more suspicious of the whole situation.

Chapter Six

"I think my grandfather knows something."

Palmer took a minute to just *breathe*. The last thing he needed was Louisa popping up at the Lariat in front of a bunch of people who would stoke whatever gossip fires were already started. But she was here, sliding in between him and the blonde on the next stool over he'd been trying to work up the interest to flirt with.

He had to look up at Louisa instead. Her green eyes were all painted up smoky and mysterious. She had bright red lipstick on and, God help him, a shirt that dipped dangerously low. Was that *glitter* all over that exposed skin?

He couldn't look. He couldn't close his eyes. She smelled like wildflowers and honey in the midst of a cold, townie bar whose Christmas decorations were all "Mele Kalikimaka"– themed here in the middle of rural Wyoming, like that made sense.

He thought about bull drool after a hard ride.

The smell of the high school locker room after a rainy football game. That time he'd cut his hand on a rusty nail in a fence and needed stitches.

Anything, *anything* but all the things he noticed about Louisa. He took a long swig of his beer. "What are you doing here?"

"I'm meeting Anna. Mostly because I figured you'd be here." She gave the beer in front of him a long, considering look. "Skipping out on the hard stuff?"

He flashed a grin at her. "Just to start, sweetheart."

She didn't roll her eyes like he'd anticipated, and maybe hoped for. Instead, she frowned a little. Almost like she was *concerned*.

"What do you want from me, Louisa?" he muttered, looking back down at his beer and wishing he had ordered that whiskey he'd been pondering.

But it had felt *wrong* to sit here and flirt and get drunk and do his *usual* when Louisa had a secret compartment and an angry grandfather.

Now she was here.

She lowered her voice, leaning in close, and he did *not* look at her. He kept his gaze on the beer. "Look into my grandfather," she said. "Something isn't right there. He acted weird. My mom acted weird about him acting weird. Maybe…"

"Maybe *what*?"

When she didn't speak, he felt compelled to glance at her and hated that she looked hurt by the snap in his tone.

"I don't know *maybe what*," she said, her voice cool and quiet. "That's the whole problem. *I* don't know how to pick a lock, but I get the feeling you won't be coming to help me with that anytime soon."

He tightened his grip on the bottle. "I said I'd help you."

"Yes, but you're making it increasingly clear you don't *want* to help." He could tell she was trying to sound…snippy or strong or whatever, but it wasn't working. She was struggling under the weight of too many what-ifs to kick his ass. So, her voice wobbled.

He felt two inches tall. "It's not about *not* wanting to help. It's about not wanting to be around you, Louisa." And damn, did that come out *all* wrong.

She looked like he'd reached out and slapped her. Her face even went a little white, which made all that glitter somehow shine brighter. "Well, fine," she muttered, whirling away from him as if she was about to storm off.

He knew how it looked. He knew how not to overreact. But he simply couldn't let her stalk off and apologize later. He couldn't let that hurt settle inside her for a second longer. So he reached for her arm before she could move away and gently pulled her back to face him.

"Don't be mad at me. Think about why that might be. *Really* think."

"What the hell are you two doing?" Anna's voice demanded from behind him.

Palmer wondered if he'd actually died a few days back and been sent to hell. He didn't immediately drop Louisa's arm. That would look like he was guilty.

He didn't have a damn thing to be guilty about, which was half the frustration. He gently released Louisa and turned to his angry sister. She was dressed just about as inappropriately as Louisa.

Okay, inappropriate wasn't *fair*. They were grown woman who could wear what they wanted. He just didn't know why he had to be in the vicinity of any of it. Particularly when half the guys in the bar were watching his *sister* with *that* look in their eyes.

"Your friend is annoying the hell out of me, so I was returning the favor," Palmer said. He didn't look to see Louisa's reaction. Couldn't let himself. "Now you're here to double-team me."

"Actually…" Anna replied, her anger already replaced by something else. Something that had

Palmer frowning. "Karma must have stepped in and done it for me."

"Huh?"

"I saw your truck in the lot. All lopsided. Tire's flat."

Palmer swore under his breath, but it suited his mood and his luck of late. It was a good enough excuse to leave the bar and not witness whatever Louisa and Anna had up their sleeves.

Anna started dragging Louisa over to a booth and Palmer made a concentrated effort not to look at her, even though he could feel her gaze on his back. He paid his tab, a piddly one beer, and tried not to feel the stares of everyone in the bar who knew him and wondered why Palmer Hudson might come by for only *one* beer and leave long before ten.

Particularly after a slightly too heated conversation with Louisa O'Brien.

He really needed to get himself out of this mess. He pushed outside into the frigid December air—which had him thinking about Louisa's outfit all over again. What did she want to do? Catch her death of cold?

Not your problem.

If only that voice in his head was half as firm and determined as it should be. He trudged over to his truck in the gravel parking lot, then stopped a few feet away. Because from the faint glow of the bar he could see what Anna hadn't been able to.

A tire on his pickup wasn't flat. All four tires had been slashed. Cut to ribbons, really.

Palmer looked around the dark parking lot. It'd be easy to do something like this without anyone seeing. But who would do it? And why?

He looked right next to his pickup where Louisa's truck was parked. The O'Briens' Orchards logo right there on the side.

He couldn't picture Greg O'Brien out here slashing his tires, but he didn't know what else this purposeful, pointed outburst of anger could be about. *Particularly* with Louisa's truck parked right here.

Palmer let out a long sigh and then pulled his phone out of his pocket. Much as he wanted to deal with this himself, he was enough of a sheriff's brother to know he needed to call the police.

Great.

"WHAT IS *WITH* YOU?"

Louisa blinked across the booth at her friend, realizing she'd been staring at the door wondering how Palmer was going to deal with his flat tire. Wondering a few too many things about Palmer instead of listening to Anna recount her latest PI case.

"I know you can get a little gooey-eyed about Palmer, but this is taking it a step too far."

"I am not gooey-eyed about Palmer," Louisa replied, more knee-jerk than anything. It wasn't about her usual Palmer flights of fancy.

Well, mostly.

Think about why that might be. Really think.

He hadn't made it sound like he didn't want to be around her because she was annoying or he hated her. He'd made it sound...

She had to push the thought away. She was sitting here with her best friend, and that was where her concentration had to be.

"What were you guys talking about all serious then? I can't remember the last time I've seen him in such a foul mood." Her eyes narrowed. "Were you two texting this morning?"

Louisa hesitated. Because she *had* been texting with Palmer, but she didn't know why that would be of any importance to Anna.

"If you are hooking up with my brother, at least have the decency to tell me."

"I'm not hooking up with anyone." At least that was the truth. She didn't want to lie to Anna. She didn't even want to keep this secret from Anna. She just knew... Anna would sweep in. She'd demand answers and justice. There would be no careful computer searches or snooping through her father's office. Anna ran on emotion, and in just about every aspect of her life, Louisa admired that about her best friend.

But she just couldn't let Anna's impulsiveness into this one. Not until she knew for sure. One way or another. "Anna. I need you to do me a huge favor."

Anna's brow furrowed. "What?"

"I need you not to worry about or ask about anything to do with Palmer for the next few weeks. Okay? I promise, after that, I'll explain everything."

Anna opened her mouth to no doubt promise, but Louisa knew her friend.

"Don't snoop around trying to figure this out. I promise I'll tell you everything. I just need time."

"You know I hate a cryptic mystery, Louisa."

"Yeah, I do know that. I'm asking you, as my best friend in the whole world, to suck it up and deal."

Anna snorted a laugh at that as she slumped back into the booth. "You don't play fair."

"That's why we're such good friends."

Anna laughed again. "All right. I promise. For two weeks. *Tops.*"

Louisa smiled thinly. Great. Now she had a time limit. Palmer would *love* that. Before she could say anything else, or change the subject to a safer one, she saw the telltale flash of red and blue lights out the bar's window.

"What do you think that's about?" she wondered aloud.

Anna twisted in the booth to look out the window and frowned. "I don't know, but look… There's Palmer."

There he was. Standing under the light outside by the entrance, little swirls of snow around him as he spoke to Chloe Brink, one of Sunrise's deputies. His arms were crossed over his chest, and he looked…furious.

Louisa hadn't realized she'd slid out of the booth to stand until Anna did the same.

"Come on," Anna said. "Let's go see what the big oaf has gotten himself into."

Louisa trailed after Anna, knowing it was none of her business. It was freezing outside, and she'd left her coat in her truck.

Yes, on the off chance Palmer might *look*.

Think about why that might be. Really think.

When they stepped outside, both Palmer and Deputy Brink turned to study them.

"Tires were slashed," he said, jerking his chin toward his pickup. There was another deputy with a flashlight inspecting the damage, so Louisa could see it wasn't just a flat tire as Anna had thought, and not even simply slashed like Palmer had said.

They were cut to ribbons. A kind of violently angry display that didn't make sense. Not in Sunrise, even at a sometimes-rowdy townie bar.

"Finally ticked off the wrong woman, huh?" Anna said. It was an attempt at humor, but Louisa saw the firm, angry disapproval on her friend's face. Anna might like to mess with Palmer, but that didn't mean she liked anyone else messing with him.

"Something like that." When Louisa looked back at his expression, and it was serious and focused on *her*, Louisa realized... He thought it connected to what was going on with *her*.

"Is that what you think happened?" Deputy Brink asked. "Pissed someone off lately?" She held a pen poised over a notebook.

"I don't know what happened, Deputy," Palmer drawled. "Because I wasn't out here. And no one came and announced their intentions or motivations to me."

Louisa wanted to chastise him for being snippy with Chloe when the woman was only doing her job, but she saw a barely leashed fury under Palmer's composed expression that she was... Not afraid of, exactly. But wary of.

"We'll take pictures. Ask a few questions. If you think of anyone who might have something against you, we can look into it..."

"But you won't find anything and mostly it'll all disappear. No answers found."

Deputy Brink stiffened, her expression bland as she flipped her notebook shut. "Your brother is the sheriff, Palmer. I'm betting it won't just disappear."

That didn't seem to change his mind on the matter. "I wouldn't bet anything serious on it," he muttered. "Thanks for coming out anyway."

Deputy Brink nodded stiffly then walked over to Palmer's truck to discuss something with the other deputy.

He turned to Anna. "Guess you're going to have to cut your night on the town short and drive me home. Unless you want to drag Mary out to pick me up."

"Why can't you just sit in the bar and get drunk like you usually do?" Anna replied.

"Because I don't really feel like having *fun* after my tires have been slashed, thanks."

Anna heaved a sigh. "Fine," she grumbled. Anna turned to Louisa. "You mind taking care of my tab?"

"Yeah, no worries. You two go. We'll figure out another night to go out." She gave Anna a quick hug then glanced at Palmer. His gaze was still dark, angry, and she didn't know...*anything* about what was going on in that brain of his, but she was happy to scurry inside and get away from the way it made her nervous. When her feelings for him rarely made her *nervous.* Embarrassed? Sure. Uncomfortable? Sometimes. Angry? Most of the time.

Nervous? It did not make *any* sense.

At the bar, she settled her and Anna's tab and while she waited to get her credit card back, her phone chimed. She looked down at the text.

From Palmer.

Figure out a way to come to the ranch tonight.

Her heart should not *flutter* about that. This was serious. Tire slashings and hidden desk compartments and her grandfather's odd behavior. None of it was about her and Palmer.

None of it would *ever* be about her and Palmer.

This was actually far more important. So she pocketed her credit card and hurried outside. Anna and Palmer were getting into Anna's car, but Anna hadn't shut her door yet. "Anna! Wait!"

Anna paused and Louisa jogged over. "Hey, I was just thinking. I could follow you to the ranch. We can still hang out. Have a girls' night in." Louisa expressly did not look at Palmer, because she knew she would...well, reveal *something*. And Anna would see it.

"Oh, well, that's a great idea," Anna agreed. "Sure, come on out."

"Why doesn't she ride with us?" Palmer said. "Maybe this was all random and someone did something to her tires too. Her truck is right next to mine. No point in getting out in the dark and cold and making sure."

Anna frowned, but when she looked over at Louisa, it wasn't with any kind of accusation. "Much as I hate to admit it, he's right. We don't know exactly what's going on. Hop in, Lou. We'll get it sorted in the morning."

Louisa wished she could believe that.

Chapter Seven

Palmer left Anna and Louisa in the living room trying to talk Mary into making and drinking margaritas with them.

He wanted to talk to Louisa privately, but more, he'd wanted to make sure she was safe. He couldn't think of a single person who'd slash his tires like that. Sure, he'd made a few women angry in his day as Anna had suggested, but he hadn't done anything to anyone that would prompt such a response. In fact, it had been a while since he'd done much more than needle his brothers and drink at home. The only thing he'd done to ruffle any feathers of late was to be caught with Louisa at the O'Briens'.

He still didn't think her grandfather was behind this. A missing birth record, a hidden desk cubby, a suspicious-acting grandfather...

Well, it added up to *something*. He hoped, for Louisa's sake, it wasn't what she thought it was. But it was *something*, so he just couldn't...let her get in that truck and drive home alone. He'd had to make sure she was safe.

So, while Louisa and his sisters did their thing. He went to his computer room and set about doing some research on Greg O'Brien. Even if he'd had nothing to do with the truck, his behavior was strange, and Louisa had asked him to look into her own grandfather.

This didn't go any better than his initial investigation. He got more and more frustrated that he couldn't find anything *remotely* shady. Not even a speeding ticket. The O'Briens weren't baby-stealing criminals. Why was he beating his head against this ridiculous brick wall when she could just ask her damn parents why there was no hospital birth record?

He pushed away from the desk, determined to head up to his room and just forget this whole thing until morning. He was running on next-to-no sleep and nothing but irritation. And he still would have to deal with whatever Jack's reaction to the slashed tires was going to be.

Instead, when he walked into the hallway, Louisa was standing there. Just *standing*.

She was still wearing that getup from the bar. All skintight jeans and low-cut top and makeup meant to make a man think of things he should not be thinking about with Louisa O'Brien.

"I didn't find anything on your grandfather,"

he said. Because that's all this was about. Not how she glittered like some kind of mirage that was real enough to touch. For someone else. Never him.

She held his gaze and nodded solemnly. "I guess I figured you wouldn't." She tried to smile. Her mouth curved, but it didn't reach her eyes. "I guess I should just…ask or leave it. We're not getting anywhere." She was trying valiantly to act like it didn't matter.

He could see through all those attempts, the cracks in her armor. Because so often he was trying that hard too.

"Maybe we should check out that hidden cubby before we ask or give up," he suggested gruffly, even though he'd just been considering giving up entirely. He just couldn't stand that look of defeat on her face.

She looked so surprised, and hopeful, he wanted…to make it all right for her. Somehow.

He moved closer so they weren't speaking across the space of a hallway, and she moved closer too. Bringing the smell of honey and alcohol with her.

Her cheeks were a little flushed when she looked up at him. "You drunk?" he asked suspiciously.

"No." He eyed her, but she didn't waver or say anything goofy. She rolled her eyes at his careful study. "One margarita is hardly going to put me flat on my face. Especially the way Mary makes them."

"You're a lightweight though."

"How would you know?"

"I know far too many things about you." You'd think he was the one drinking, saying senseless things like that. Like what he'd said at the bar. When he'd never even finished his beer.

She just stood there, but her eyes studied him. Like, if she stared enough, she could read every thought in his head. He had the uncomfortable sensation she might be able to do just that.

Still he just stood there. Looking right back because… She was beautiful. And strong and smart and he *wanted* her. Even if he didn't *want* to want her.

"Palmer. Back at the bar you said—"

He wasn't sure he could stand to hear his own words used against him. "I say a lot of things."

She nodded slowly. "I suppose you don't always say what you mean. But I think you meant what you said, but *I* don't understand what it meant. Because as far as I can tell, as far as you always treat me, you think I'm still just a pesky little kid."

"You're pesky all right." But she was determined. He could see it in the glint in her eyes. In the way she stood there, clearly deciding not to back down. To poke at this…and then what? What good could come from it?

"When you're with me, when you're around me, do you think of me as a kid? Or not?" she asked.

A kid. When she was dressed like that. When her casual touch made his body tight, and her laugh made him feel like he'd won every event in the rodeo. He'd wanted to touch her for too long now, a desperation that only seemed to grow. He couldn't stem the tide. He couldn't avoid her enough lately to avoid thinking about her.

"I've had just about everyone in a fifty-mile radius warn me off you this week," he said even though it didn't answer her question. Because it was a reminder. Of who they were, and how his wants did not matter.

No one wanted wild, irresponsible Palmer Hudson messing with sweet, upstanding Louisa O'Brien.

"Since when do you listen to anyone?" she replied.

It wasn't just a challenge. It was a statement of fact. He didn't listen to anyone. He did what he pleased, much as he could. He shouldn't, when it came to Louisa, except she seemed to have a few of her own wants.

He…could fulfill them. She was right there.

Standing within reach. Why was he trying so hard to be…noble or good or right, when literally *no one* expected anything like that of him. If he touched her, if he kissed her… It didn't have to mean…

They both jolted at the sound of a phone jangling. He watched her hands shake as she pulled her phone out of her pocket—which gratified him even when it shouldn't. She frowned.

"It's my mom. She should be in bed." She turned away from him, drawing the phone to her ear. "Mom? It's late. Is everything o—" The noise she made instead of finishing the question was one of pure anguish. "I'll be right there," she managed to say in a choked rush, already moving past Palmer.

"Lou—"

"I have to go. The house is on fire."

PALMER HAD DRIVEN HER. Louisa had been too shaken up and everyone had insisted someone else drive. Anna had sat in the back of the car, holding her hand and whispering assurances.

Everything that happened in that hallway had fallen by the wayside because her mother had been crying. *Crying.* Her mother who'd saw off her own limbs before she cried in front of Louisa—or anyone.

Louisa could see the flashing emergency

lights from the highway as Palmer pulled onto the drive that would wind around to the house. Her heart was in her throat, and everything was just…wrong.

Because the closer they got to the house, the more she could see. The house. Engulfed in big, huge flames that didn't make any sense.

She heard Anna swear next to her, but she was in a kind of fog. Everything felt cottony even as she stared at the sight before her as Palmer pulled to a stop.

The home she'd grown up in. Her father and grandfather had grown up in. Flames and black soot and a firetruck working to arc a big blast of water at the blaze while the stars and moon glittered above.

The water was too late. She could see that even not knowing anything about fire. It had taken over everything.

It was all too late.

Palmer opened the back door. When she didn't move, he held out a hand. "Come on, Lou. Let's go find your parents."

It was the word *parents* that got her moving. And Palmer's hand. It was an actionable part of this whole thing. Take Palmer's hand. Find her parents. Step by step through…whatever nightmare this was.

His hand was larger than hers and firm. He

didn't let her balk at what she saw. He led her right to her parents.

Mom was still crying. Dad was pale as the moonlight. When they registered that she was there, they both moved toward her and enveloped her in a hug. She lost Palmer's hand somewhere along the way, but her parents were holding her. Crying.

So she cried too.

"Thank God for those darn dogs," Dad said, his voice scratchy—from smoke or emotion or both. "They kept up a racket until we got out of bed to see what was the matter."

Louisa's heart felt as though it stopped for a full minute. Her parents had been asleep and a fire had started and… She hugged them tighter.

"What happened?" she managed to ask after a while, still holding them close, one arm around each parent.

"We don't know," Dad said. "We just got out and called 9-1-1."

They all surveyed the many emergency services and personnel around them. Firefighters and cops and an ambulance. Thank God no one had needed the latter.

Still, it was clear there would be nothing left of the house. Nothing left…

"We can stay at your grandparents'," Mom was saying. "We'll…rebuild." She struggled with the word, and Louisa struggled to believe in *rebuilding* in the midst of all this destruction. But the orchard itself seemed safe. It was only the house that had been affected, hopefully. It had been an unfortunate accident and her parents and their dogs had survived.

That was all that mattered.

She looked around and didn't realize she was looking for Palmer until she'd found him in the crowd. Both he and Anna stood with one of the officers, talking.

It all felt a bit like a nightmare and there was the distant hope she'd just…wake up. And it would all go away. But the firefighters continued to contain the blaze. Friends came as news spread through town and the sun began to rise. There were offers of places to stay, clothes to wear. Food.

Everyone in Sunrise would rally around them and everything would be fine. A house was just a house. Things were replaceable.

She didn't let herself think about the strange secret cubby in her father's desk, because none of that mattered anymore. She wouldn't let it. Kyla Brown and missing sisters were someone else's problem.

Her parents were her parents. Her grandfather had been acting strangely because Palmer had been with her—and as Palmer had said, people were warning him off her right and left. Palmer, who was a genius with computers, hadn't found anything. The *singular* missing hospital record was a mistake. A fluke.

This was over. She needed to call Palmer to tell him so. No doubt he and Anna had gone home at some point.

Before she could take out her phone, she saw both of them. Still there. Plus Jack and Mary. Jack and Anna were talking to some of the firefighters. Mary was talking to a small group of neighbors, and Louisa could tell even from all the way over here that she was organizing things.

Louisa wanted to simply sink into the ground and cry some more, but she knew her parents would worry. She needed to be strong for them. And she needed to tell Palmer this was all over.

She searched the rest of the yard then saw him a ways off, filling the dogs' water dishes. Louisa swallowed at the lump in her throat. Those dogs had saved her parents' lives.

Mom and Dad were deep in a conversation with Reverend Plumber that Louisa had only been half listening to.

"I'll be right back," Louisa whispered to Mom, giving her arm a squeeze before heading toward Palmer.

He watched her approach, and she realized

he'd brought food and treats for the dogs. It wasn't just that he'd been giving them water, he was taking care of them.

She was going to cry all over again.

"We'll take these guys back to the ranch for a bit until you guys get settled somewhere. Mary's organizing everything. Clothes, food, you name it. You've got the whole town behind you and your folks."

Louisa nodded. It echoed all her thoughts and, what's more, proved her point. She had a good life. Great parents. An amazing community that would rally around tragedy. Why had she been about tearing that at the foundations?

"I just wanted to let you know that I'm done," she managed to grit out, every word a fight through her tightened throat.

His expression went to confused. "What?"

"I don't want to look into the whole dumb Brown family missing sister anymore. My parents are my parents and that's that. It was foolish, and I'm done. Thank you for helping me and keeping it a secret. Really. But I was wrong."

He reached out. He put his hand on her shoulder and gave it a squeeze. "Lou, it's been a day. Let's not jump to—"

"No. I'm done. I'm *done*. It's over. The end."

He blinked and she could *feel* all the ways he didn't approve, which didn't make sense. It made her angry. Which was better than all this terrible dismay. Still, he didn't argue with her. She kind of wanted him to. She wanted to have a fight.

His hand slid down her back. Then he gave it a rub up and down. Like he was trying to calm someone hysterical.

She wasn't though. She was *done*.

"Ed's heading over to your parents. Let's go hear what he has to say, okay?"

She wanted to argue with him. Shove his hand away from her. Or she thought she should want that, but she just…let him steer her back to her parents. His hand on her back like some kind of guiding force.

Ed Connolly, the fire chief, was standing in front of her parents, and as she approached, he nodded to her and Palmer.

"I'm real sorry this happened, and that we couldn't do more to save the structure," he offered. He wasn't covered in soot, like some of his men, but his face was red like he'd done some hard physical work.

"It's all right, Ed. We know you did the best you could," Dad said, still sounding raspy. But the EMTs had checked her parents out and said they were fine.

Louisa held on to that like a talisman.

"I appreciate that, Tim. Unfortunately, I've

got a little more bad news. We're going to have to bring in a fire investigator. We don't have one in Sunrise. So we'll have to reach out to the county and go from there."

"What?" Mom and Dad said in unison.

"Why?" Louisa and Palmer asked together.

"I'm sorry, folks. But everything we saw in there makes it look like someone set this. Deliberately."

Chapter Eight

Palmer hadn't been surprised by Ed's conclusion, though he could tell Louisa and her parents were. It was just too big a fire. Too out of control too fast in the middle of all this cold and snow.

Then there was the timing. Everything had started going bad once he and Louisa had found that hidden compartment. It didn't make any sense yet, but he'd make sense of it one way or another. Whether Louisa liked it or not.

She was in danger until they got to the bottom of whatever was going on.

Unfortunately, the whole past twenty-four hours made Louisa's grandfather look guilty as sin since he'd been the one who'd caught them in the office. And, according to Louisa, had never explained why he'd been there when he'd thought the house would be empty.

Now, the night after the fire, Louisa was staying under her grandfather's roof. Palmer had tried to carefully influence Anna to convince

Louisa to stay at the Hudson Ranch, but Anna had insisted Louisa should be with her family and then started questioning why he was so invested. She hadn't been exactly wrong on the family point. Louisa *should* be with her parents, no doubt. He wasn't about to touch Anna's questioning about *motive* with a million-foot pole.

So he'd tried a more direct approach—*tried* being the operative word because Louisa refused to answer his calls or respond to his texts. He understood it, to an extent. She was in the midst of emotional upheaval and didn't want any more. And since the only thing she'd wanted him for was to help her solve a mystery, she didn't need to talk to him.

Maybe that bothered him, if he thought too deeply about it, but he wasn't one for thinking deeply. He was one for *acting*. So he had to take some things into his own hands.

He wasn't delusional enough to think Louisa would ever thank him, but he knew it needed to be done. It was the right thing to do. If she wouldn't look out for herself, he would.

He did another search on both of her parents in between some research for Grant's current case. Then spent a late evening poring over Greg O'Brien's life.

When that didn't yield anything to go on, he went back to Louisa's hospital records he *could* find. Then he dug around in his own family files until he found Anna's birth and hospital records. Louisa and Anna had been born in the same year, if not the same month. Maybe comparing what information Anna's records had and Louisa's didn't would yield some kind of lightbulb moment.

At first, there was nothing really. Just his sister's birth information. His parents' information. But tucked into the formal records of Anna's first days was a notebook piece of paper labeled "Thank Yous." There were about thirty names—all divided into sections—in his mother's perfect, precise handwriting. There were tiny checkmarks next to each name, presumably after his mother had written and sent the thank-you letters off.

It took his breath away for a minute. Not unusual. It didn't matter how much time had passed, there were always sneaky and unexpected things that slipped under all his defenses and turned him for a moment in time back to that twelve-year-old who couldn't comprehend his mother wasn't coming back.

He held very still, and breathed very carefully, waiting for the wave of pain and grief to wash through and leave a kind of emptiness in its wake. That was how this went. Because Mom had been gone more than she'd been in his life, and there was nothing he could do about it.

He read every category of names, out loud in a whisper to anchor himself to the here and now.

Family. Friends. Ranch. Doctors & Nurses.

Doctors & Nurses. They would have all worked at the hospital, and if they'd been around for Anna's birth, likely most had been around at the time of Louisa's too. Maybe one of them remembered something. An explanation of why the paperwork was missing.

For good or for ill. It was a small town; even Harvey, where the hospital was, wasn't a thriving metropolis. Maybe someone there would remember.

And if this somehow tied to slashed tires and fires...

He heard the doorknob turn and quickly slid the list of names back into the file. He didn't try to shove the file back in its place. That would look too obviously like he was trying to hide something. So he turned and tried very hard not to scowl at Jack standing there.

"What's up?" Palmer asked, doing his best to sound casual. He even tried to smile, but doubted it landed.

"Grant said you'd found everything he asked for. I was just wondering why you're still holed up in here when it's dinnertime."

Palmer shrugged. "Lost track of time, I guess."

Jack drifted closer, frowning at the closed folder on the desk. And where the filing cabinet was open to.

"Why are you looking at family stuff?"

"I was looking for something of mine, but I got distracted." He opened Anna's file, pointed at the painful and wonderful memory of his mother. "Anytime I think Mary's as meticulous as they come, I remember she got it all from Mom."

Jack's expression didn't change, but he didn't say anything for long ticking moments as he looked at the list in Mom's handwriting. Maybe his face didn't outwardly show any emotion, but Palmer had a sneaking suspicion when his brother did that very still, silent thing, he was pushing down whatever complicated emotions he *did* feel.

Jack finally looked up from the list and met Palmer's eyes. "I know you're hiding something. I don't appreciate secrets, Palmer."

Palmer struggled with a flash of temper. Maybe it was what felt like his mother's ghost that kept him from lashing out at his brother. Maybe it was something closer to maturity. He didn't know and didn't want to examine it to find out.

Besides, this wasn't about him. It was about

Louisa. He wouldn't let Jack in on that when she was so dead set against it. Particularly *now* when she didn't even want him to keep looking into this whole thing. "Let's just say, I'm not keeping my own secrets. Okay?"

He didn't expect Jack's acceptance of that. Jack wasn't known for understanding or respecting his siblings' boundaries. Jack was a demanding bulldozer.

"I suppose that's fair."

"You do?"

Jack scowled. "Dinner is ready. Come eat. You can deal with whatever this is later."

Palmer was very reluctant to leave it be. He wanted to press on, but his older brother's goodwill would only extend so far. So he left the file where it was and followed Jack to the dining room. Grant was helping Mary put food on the table while Dahlia and Anna chatted in low tones. He could hear Cash and Izzy coming in through the back, stomping off snow, the dogs yipping in excitement behind them.

They all gathered around the table, just like they would have done when they were kids. When Dad sat where Jack took his seat. When Mom was the one serving dinner. Before Grant had gone to war or Izzy had been born. A lifetime ago, and Palmer missed it. He did.

But in this strange moment, looking back in

time for Louisa, knowing she'd just lost every material thing, he was grateful. So grateful his family had somehow weathered the storms and could come to eat dinner together. Night after night.

He was lucky, in a lot of ways.

So he ate dinner with his family, and he enjoyed it. He let himself be present. Laugh and eat. Clean up afterward with Cash and Izzy. Tease and enjoy his niece who would be a teenager the next time he damn well blinked.

He'd been thinking about getting older lately, but this solidified something inside him. Not just that he wasn't precisely *young* anymore, but that he really needed to figure out what was next. What he wanted out of his life. Coasting could only get a man so far, and he'd coasted long enough.

He sat in his office later that night, setting about to track down all the doctors and nurses who might know something about Louisa's birth. Determined to find answers for her.

And figure out some answers when it came to Louisa O'Brien for himself.

LOUISA SPENT THE days after the fire running herself ragged to help her parents in whatever way she could. She struggled to sleep in her grandparents' little house in town. She struggled to force herself to eat. So she kept herself busy. She kept herself focused.

When Mary and Anna encouraged her to take a break, she refused. When Palmer called and texted…she ignored it.

She just…didn't want to deal with him. She could fall apart in front of Anna or Mary without feeling embarrassed. Without feeling raw. They were her friends. They'd been through everything together.

Palmer was just…the man she'd trusted with a really personal secret. She could not for the life of her face him until she felt less like a dandelion that had been blown to hell.

She drove up to her grandparents' house after running to the pharmacy for her dad. It had been an emotional gauntlet of everyone she passed or interacted with wanting to wish her and her family well. To tell her how terrible it was, but how resilient they'd be and rebuild.

She knew that. She didn't need anyone to tell her. She *knew* everyone was just trying to be nice, to help and offer words of encouragement, but she wanted to cover her ears and run away.

Instead she'd smiled and issued thank-yous and somehow collected her father's blood pressure medication and then driven back to her grandparents' house. When she parked her car, she just sat there for a moment. There was a pickup with the fire department logo on it—Ed the fire chief's. Next to it, a slick sedan that she didn't recognize.

She sat there. Still gripping the steering wheel even though her truck was in Park. She forced herself to breathe slowly, in and out. She'd handle whatever this was. She had to.

For her family.

So, she got out and headed in, her father's prescription in her purse. When she stepped inside, she heard voices in the living room and turned toward them.

Arranged in her grandparents' cramped gathering room was her parents, both Grandma and Grandpa, Ed and a man she didn't know, no doubt the owner of that car outside. The man wore a suit and looked…cruel. She didn't know why that descriptor popped into her head, but the perception of him made her pause in the entrance to the living room.

Dad waved her in, and Mom pointed to her. "This is our daughter. She also lives in the house."

The man's cold gaze turned to her and he offered her a nod. "Ma'am. I'm Investigator Steele. I have a few questions for you and your family."

"Of course," Louisa acknowledged. There was nowhere left to sit, so she stood where she was in the entry.

"Is there any reason you have to believe someone might wish your family harm?" the investigator asked of no one in particular. Like he was testing to see who would answer.

She thought of Palmer. Grandpa's strange behavior. The Facebook messages from Kyla Brown.

All. Your. Fault.

"I can't think of a single person who'd want to hurt us," Mom said firmly.

"Maybe business competition?" Mr. Steele offered.

"We don't really have much competition around here," Dad returned, looking pale and white and *unwell*. "We're all too spread out."

The investigator made a little note on his pad. He looked up at her. Louisa felt like there was a big red word stamped across her face: *guilty*.

"I can't think of a single person," she managed to croak. "The town has rallied around us. Helped in every way they can. Mom and Dad are involved in the community and are always helping people. We hold community events at the orchard, and we've never had problems bigger than a teenage tussle or someone sneaking off with someone they shouldn't and getting caught—which never had anything to do with *us*. If someone set that fire on purpose, it must have been some kind of misunderstanding."

"That's quite a speech," the investigator said. The remark *felt* sarcastic, but there was really no inflection to how he said the words.

"Louisa? Is that Palmer's truck?" Mom pointed out the window where Palmer's pickup was indeed pulling into the driveway.

"I think so."

"Must have gotten his tires fixed then," Dad commented. "Why don't you go out and tell him we're a bit busy with Mr. Steele here."

Louisa nodded even though she didn't want to deal with Palmer. She also didn't want to deal with the way the investigator was staring at her. She turned and went back outside.

She hesitated on the porch. There had to be some way to get rid of him without having to have a private conversation. If she stayed this close to the porch, maybe she could just say they were busy.

He got out of his truck. He had his cowboy hat on, and his expression was grim. Apparently, he hadn't taken her ignoring his calls or texts too well. Still, he looked handsome and capable in the afternoon sun, and there was some small part of her that wanted to run to him and lay it all on his shoulders.

The door behind her opened and the investigator stepped out, reminding her of all the ways that wasn't an option.

"Boyfriend?"

She looked up at the investigator, eyebrows drawn together. It didn't sound in the least bit flirtatious, but how exactly would that relate to an investigation? "Just a friend. Why?"

Mr. Steele shrugged. "You never know who might take thwarted feelings out on somebody."

Louisa felt her cheeks heat. "There are no… thwarted feelings." She thought about what Palmer had said at the bar, that moment in the Hudson hallway before everything had fallen apart. Where she'd thought…maybe he didn't look at her and see a little kid at *all*.

That didn't matter now. The investigator was jotting something down on his notebook page as Palmer crossed the yard. When Mr. Steele finished writing, he looked at her and he smiled. He didn't seem *quite* so cruel when he smiled, but she still had an incredibly *off* feeling about this man.

Still, politeness was so deeply ingrained in her, she smiled back. "Thank you for everything you're doing to get to the bottom of this, Mr. Steele. My family appreciates it."

He nodded then handed her a business card he pulled from the back of his notebook. "If you think of anything or anyone who might have something to prove, just give me a call. Either way, I'll be getting to the bottom of things."

His delivery was so dry, so devoid of anything resembling inflection, she didn't know if that was some kind of attempt at comfort or a threat.

He walked away. Down the porch stairs and toward his car. He didn't say anything to Palmer as they crossed paths. Just nodded. Palmer nodded back with a puzzled expression on his face.

When he reached her, he didn't crest the stairs. He stood at the bottom and looked up at her. "Who was that?"

Chapter Nine

Palmer did not recognize the hot, angry ball of emotion sitting in his chest. It had popped up when the fancy suit had smiled down at Louisa.

And she'd smiled back.

Now it sat there, an uncomfortable burning sensation that he didn't know what to do with, but knew he needed to keep it to himself.

"The fire investigator," Louisa finally said, her eyes on the man as he got in his car and then reversed out of the driveway.

Palmer tried very hard not to scowl, because he had a very sinking feeling the emotion assailing him was *jealousy*. When he'd never been jealous a day in his life and had no reason to start now. He'd just promised himself to behave maturely, not get all caveman over a woman who wasn't even involved with him.

Much as you'd like to change that.

He scowled at the voice in his head. So, maybe he would. Didn't mean now was the time. Or that Louisa wanted anything to do with him. Oh, sure, she'd made it clear in that hallway and a few times over the past year she was *attracted*.

Attracted didn't mean much when a man had the reputation he did. Didn't matter what had come over him in the past few days, maturity or some kind of head injury, if he was even considering something with Louisa, it would not be the same kind of one-night stand he was used to.

Not only because he was pretty sure eighty-five percent of the town would conspire to murder him.

"Should an investigator be hitting on one of the victims?" Okay, that was not a mature or reasonable way to conduct himself. Maybe he was a lost cause.

"He wasn't hitting on me," she replied. Then her eyebrows drew together and her nose kind of scrunched up. "I don't think."

"You don't *think*?"

"Well, he asked me if you were my boyfriend. Then said something about thwarted feelings could cause people to set fires or something, which makes sense. It was just the way he asked was…weird."

Weird. Palmer looked darkly back at where the man had been…in his nice suit and fancy car. Now both gone. He turned to Louisa, arms crossed over his chest, trying so very hard to keep his voice even. "What did you say?"

"About what?"

"About me being your boyfriend?"

"That you're just a friend. You know, since you're *not* my boyfriend," she replied sharply even as her cheeks darkened toward pink.

Palmer shrugged. "I just meant because your grandpa caught us together at the house and I don't think he was buying either of our stories."

"No, but…" She blew out a breath. "He'll… figure it out. Whatever this is. Regardless of us. I know we didn't start any fires." As if it reminded her, she looked up at him. "Your tires are fixed. Any leads on that?"

He shook his head and thought about telling her to tell the investigator about it, and how he thought they might connect somehow. But he was an investigator in his own right and so was his brother. This arson guy didn't need to know everything until Palmer knew he was trustworthy enough to do the right thing with any information.

"What's the guy's name?"

She rolled her eyes. "Palmer, this is none of your business. I don't know why you're here but—"

"I'll get it out of somebody. You might as well tell me."

She huffed a breath but handed him the business card. He studied the print: Hawk Steele. Fire & Arson Investigator. Bent County, Wyoming. Palmer looked at Louisa. "That's not his real name."

"Ed seems to know him. I don't think he's a fake, Palmer. I certainly don't know why he'd have reason to lie about any of it." She held her hand out for the card, so he returned it.

He'd be looking into *Hawk Steele*, that was for sure.

For right now, it was just him and Louisa—her on the porch, him still at the staircase landing. She didn't look directly at him, instead scowling into the distance.

She didn't tell him to go or ask him why he was here. She just stood there, so he went ahead and took the stairs he hadn't stepped up when he'd arrived. She looked at him and there was a flash of something—something soft and vulnerable—before she blinked it all away.

He reached out and touched her face. Because she was building up those walls, brick by brick. Keeping everyone out while she fell apart on the inside. He knew all the signs. He'd been doing it most of his life. Her cheek was soft, and she jolted when he dragged his thumb across her cheekbone. "You're looking rough, Lou."

She jerked her face away. "Gee, thanks," she said, slapping at his hand.

"Don't be vain, now. You've been through the wringer and you're not giving yourself a break. Why don't you let someone take care of you?"

Why did he want it to be him?

"The whole town is taking care of us." She took a step away and crossed her arms over her chest like she was warding him off.

"I said *you*," Palmer replied. "You're taking care of your parents, holding it together for them, and you're not letting yourself fall apart."

She looked up at him, and her expression was all defiance, but tears glittered in those mesmerizing green eyes. "I have, in fact, cried on both your sisters' shoulders, thank you."

"Well, good." And it didn't matter that he wanted it to be *his* shoulder. That wasn't what this was about.

Or not only.

"The fact of the matter is this investigator complicates things. Maybe this fire and my tires don't connect. Maybe none of it has to do with those messages from Kyla Brown about her missing sister. But even if they don't, he's bound to stumble across them. Poke at them and see if they do."

"Are you trying to make all this worse?" she asked. So frustrated. So close to her breaking point, but it was only because she was trying so hard to compartmentalize. To keep all these little pieces separate and within her control.

He knew. He understood. As much as he'd like to be able to let her do that, he knew it didn't help anyone. He *knew* her. Whether either of them liked it or not. She needed answers, no matter how she tried to tell herself she didn't.

"No, I don't want to make anything worse for you, Lou. I'm trying to tell you we need to figure it out first. I know you… No matter what the truth is, you love your parents. You want to protect them. So let's get to the bottom of this so we can figure out *how*."

Louisa had been certain she was done. She was leaving questions of her parentage behind. Maybe it had been the trauma of the fire talking, but she'd promised herself. Because her parents had survived and not been *burned alive*, and nothing else mattered.

Nothing.

Now Palmer was putting a different perspective on the whole thing. That finding answers might be required to protect her parents.

She didn't want to cry in front of him. She didn't want to cry. There'd been enough of that. She wanted to bury her head in the sand, take care of her parents and forget literally everything else, including the fire.

"I can't…"

He shook his head and didn't let her finish. "We can. We will."

We. Because she'd asked him for his help. She'd known…there wasn't a Hudson who'd give up. Who'd let her handle this on her own. In all their own ways, they would have helped because it was who they were.

But she'd only been able to really fathom asking Palmer for help, and even now she didn't know exactly why that was. It was more than some crush she'd had since she was thirteen. It was all those feelings that had twisted and dug deep and grown roots over the course of the past few years, and these past few months especially.

He'd touched her face. He'd told her he knew too many things about her, and maybe he'd never come out and said specifically he didn't think of her as a kid, she knew he didn't.

Something had changed.

She didn't know what he was doing *here*. Touching *her* and being all nice. This wasn't his usual thing. Sweetness and out-of-his-way help. Palmer wasn't selfish, exactly, but he didn't extend an effort for anyone unless he really wanted to.

Sure, he had obligation drilled into him because he was a Hudson. But Palmer was just… different. A little bit more willing to buck the trend. Not a fan of martyring himself like his brothers were.

He'd said it himself at the bar, that he didn't like to be around her. Even if that had to do with…other things, *attraction* things if she had to name it, he was going against what he liked… for her.

"Go tell your parents I'm taking you for a drive so you can clear your head. I've got some potential leads we can talk about."

She didn't even bristle at him telling her what to do. That's how tired and brittle she felt. "You take me for a drive, they're going to think things."

He didn't even flinch. Just held her gaze, his dark eyes steady on her. "Yeah, I know."

She tried to ignore the fluttering of her heart, because… Well, a lot of becauses. "I seem to recall that bothering you. Deeply."

He didn't say anything. He in fact let the silence stretch out, which had always been Palmer's greatest strength. He didn't need to fill a silence.

She desperately *wanted* to. So much, she was doing everything she could not to fidget, down to biting her tongue. She'd spoken last. It was *his* turn.

"I can go in and tell them, if you want," he said after that long, long silence.

She scowled at him. "I don't appreciate your high-handedness, Palmer," she said as haughtily as she could manage. Bickering with him was making her feel a *little* steadier though. Almost as if he'd planned it.

His mouth curved, ever so slightly. "I'm not so sure about that, Lou."

Unfortunately, neither was she. So she whirled around and marched herself inside. Her parents were still talking with Ed, so she decided to just tell her grandmother. It'd be easier anyway.

She hoped.

"With Palmer," Grandma said, frowning after Louisa had told her. "A drive?"

"Just to kind of clear my head." She tried to smile at her grandmother, but it faltered.

Grandma's frown turned into a full-on, narrowed-eyes scowl. "Do you think I was born yesterday, young lady?"

"Wh…what?"

"You don't think I ever went for a *drive* with your grandfather." She put the word *drive* in air quotes and Louisa's face immediately heated. For *so many* reasons.

"Please don't say that."

"What? You think your father was delivered by stork?"

"Oh, my *God*, Grandma. Please don't."

"All I'm saying is any young woman getting in a car with Palmer Hudson to *clear their head* better know how to protect themselves."

"'Bye, Grandma." Louisa turned away. Good Lord. She was twenty-four years old and, as aware as she was that parents and grandparents…did things, it didn't mean she ever wanted to discuss it with them.

Ever.

She launched herself outside, causing Palmer's placid expression to go questioning. "You okay?"

She nodded. Too hard, as she started for his truck. Then she shook her head because it was ridiculous. Her reaction. The whole thing. "I think my grandma just gave me *the talk*."

Palmer, appropriately, shuddered as he came to walk beside her. "Please don't give me flashbacks."

"But…" She didn't want to come out and say all the grandparents in his life had died young, and before his parents had disappeared. He knew all that.

"Every elderly woman decided to be our honorary grandmother after Mom and Dad disappeared. The one thing people seem to remember when you don't have parents is to make sure to awkwardly lecture you about safe sex. Jack.

Cash, since he considered himself a great expert, having gotten Chessa pregnant. Mrs. Riley. Mrs. Sanders. Coach Albright."

"No."

"Oh, yes. There's probably more that I've blocked out."

He opened the passenger's-side door of the pickup for her, and she'd give him, or maybe her grandmother, credit. She'd forgotten about everything to do with the fire and her parentage for the past five minutes.

But now it all came crashing back. Because the tires to this pickup had been slashed. And the only reason she was in a truck with Palmer was that she had asked him for help. And him not backing off when she'd asked him to.

Louisa wanted to be mad about it, but she just…couldn't be as he climbed into the driver's seat. Palmer cared. Maybe it wasn't clear, to either of them, just *what* he cared about, but he cared.

And, as much as she hated to admit it, having Palmer drive her away from her grandparents' house was like taking a full breath for the first time since her mother had called her. She was being crushed from the inside out trying to keep it all together for her parents and…

Palmer reached across the center console and wrapped his fingers around hers. He squeezed her hand, his eyes still on the road. She looked down at his hand covering hers. His was big, rough. Very scarred—no doubt from ranch work and the rodeo. Maybe even those reckless football years. That was the thing about Palmer, he'd always been reckless. Flinging himself into just about anything.

Maybe that was why she'd fallen in love with him when she'd been still a girl. Why she couldn't get rid of the feelings now that she was an adult. She knew it wasn't exactly courage that had sent him punishing his body in different ways over the years. It was probably a lot of unresolved trauma, in fact.

But he wasn't *afraid*. And she had been. She'd always had the nice parents. The parents everyone wished they'd had. Wanting different for herself than they'd wanted for her had been hard. Going to college out east had been a leap into the unknown.

Because Palmer had showed her that you could, and that you could learn something from it, and the people who loved you didn't stop, even when you did something outside of the box.

She curled her own fingers around his. So that they were holding hands. A unit against whatever was out there slashing tires and setting fires. He was helping her, no matter what the truth about where she'd come from was.

Not too long ago, she'd sworn she'd rather cut off her own tongue than ever confess her feelings toward him. Not attraction, but the actual *feelings*. In this moment, she wondered if it would really be such a tragedy to tell him. "Palmer…"

Before she could find the words, something in him hardened. "Looks like we're being followed."

Chapter Ten

At first, when Palmer had noticed the nondescript sedan keeping pace on the highway, he'd wondered if it was a coincidence, or if someone was looking out for Louisa. If her grandmother had thought this was some kind of event that had necessitated a sex talk, maybe other people would too. It was a small town and people were nosy.

So, he'd taken a few strange turns. Back roads and scenic byways that no one would be following *accidentally*. Only purposefully.

And the sedan was still there. It was a Wyoming plate, but he didn't recognize the car and, no matter how he slowed, the car wouldn't get close enough for him to get a good view of the driver.

"Can you read that plate?" he asked Louisa. He dropped her hand so he could take a quick turn. At first, he'd had no destination in mind, but now he was starting to formulate a plan.

Louisa twisted in her seat and looked behind them. "No, it's too far away."

"Okay, text this to Anna." He waited for her to get her phone out of her pocket. "Got a tail. Gray Toyota Camry. Maybe a 2010 model or around there. One driver, can't make out plate except it's Wyoming. Going to lead them to Dead Man's Bluff."

Louisa quickly typed that into her phone then looked over at him. "You know, weirdly, I don't want to lead anyone anywhere near *Dead Man's* Bluff. It was fun and thrilling when I was fifteen, but these days *dead man* just feels like a threat."

"If the person following isn't local, it'll give us the advantage. We know the parking, the trailheads, the terrain. They won't," Palmer replied, turning off for the dirt patch locals considered a parking lot for the difficult hike. And that was in the summer when it wasn't packed with snow.

"And if they *are* local?" Louisa demanded as he pulled to a stop.

Palmer shrugged. "I don't recognize the car. Seems far less likely."

"So the plan is to what? Park here?"

She was sounding close to panic, so he kept himself very calm and utilized his usual careless demeanor—even if he'd never be careless with

Louisa. "No, we'll get out." He turned off the ignition, studied her clothes. She was dressed for winter, and while neither of them was prepared for a long hike in the freezing temperatures, they'd be all right for a while.

"We'll hike over to the lookout. Pretend we're..." He watched her wait for whatever word was next, and the more he waited, the redder her cheeks got.

Now was really not the time to find any sort of enjoyment out of that, but he was certainly not a saint, even if he had decided to step into maturity. "Talking," he eventually finished.

She narrowed her eyes at him but did not speak.

"We'll see what they do. Chances are, they'll drive on by. But they'll have to turn around once they get to the dead end." Palmer checked his watch. "It'll hopefully give Anna enough time to drive out this way, maybe spot the sedan and get a plate. Jack'll run it, then we'll know what's up."

"And if they don't drive right on by but stop?"

Palmer shrugged. "We'll play it by ear."

"Isn't that dangerous?"

He reached over and unlocked the glove compartment. He pulled out his holstered gun. He didn't always keep it there, but ever since his tires had been slashed, he'd figured it was smart.

"Not as dangerous as you'd think." With that, he got out of the truck and into the cold.

The temperatures were likely hovering near zero all the way up here. He hooked the holster to his belt and then pulled his coat back down over it so whoever was following them might not be able to tell he was carrying.

He skirted the bed of the pickup and went over to Louisa's side. She'd opened the door but hadn't stepped down yet. "I'm pretty sure that's a sheet of pure ice," she said, pointing to the ground below.

"Here." He moved close as he could without sliding on the patch of ice himself. He held out his arms. "Jump."

"You're out of your mind," Louisa replied.

"I'll catch you, and then you won't slip and bust your head open."

"You'll drop me and we'll likely *both* bust our heads open."

"Ye of little faith." He held out his hands again. "I used to stay on my feet with three-hundred-pound linebackers running into me."

"Yeah, that was ten years ago. You're old now."

"Louisa, I swear to God."

"Fine," she muttered. She didn't look certain, but she perched herself on the truck's running board, then reached out. Instead of jumping, she crouched and reached out until her hands were on his shoulders.

Then she kind of leaned herself into him, and he caught her weight as she wrapped arms and legs around him—clearly desperately afraid he'd drop her or topple over. He had no problem keeping his balance though.

Absolutely *no* problem having her wrapped around him like this.

It wasn't the time. Maybe never was the time. But he'd like to keep holding her just like this. Right here. Just the two of them.

He heard the faint sound of an engine. Whoever was following them was getting close. So he sighed, moved back a few steps, then let her down on safer, less slick ground.

She didn't pull her arms from around his shoulders, and he didn't take his hands off her hips. In the bright winter afternoon, they stood there and looked at each other. Much like they had in that hallway just a few nights ago.

Palmer was well aware he should say something. Confess *any* of the feelings he had, yet his throat felt dry. He usually knew how to throw himself headfirst into just about anything, but this?

"They're pulling in," she said softly the second before her gaze left his and went to some point behind him.

Palmer turned slowly, sliding his arm around Louisa's waist. He'd keep playing the role of two lovers who'd gone on a drive for a little privacy. Even if it didn't feel so much like *playing* right now.

As he turned, he sighed heavily as he recognized the man behind the wheel.

"It's the fire investigator," Louisa said.

So Palmer went ahead and swore.

LOUISA DIDN'T KNOW why the sight of Hawk Steele made her more nervous than some nameless stranger, but her stomach tied itself in knots. Why on earth had he followed them? And he'd changed cars.

None of it felt good or right. Surely this wasn't procedure. Louisa was just enough worried about this man that when Palmer angled his body in front of hers, like he was protecting her from Mr. Steele, she let him.

"Mr. Hudson," the fire investigator said. "I just need to ask you a few questions."

"So you *followed us here*? In a different car than you had before?"

Mr. Steele took his sweet time to look from Palmer over to her, still almost hidden behind Palmer's tall, broad frame. "Yes."

"Why on earth do you need him to answer any questions?" Louisa demanded before

Palmer said anything. Because this was ludi-
crous. Palmer didn't have anything to do with
this.

The man's blue fathomless gaze held hers.
"Matter of course," he said without inflection.

Louisa stepped forward, ready to push Palmer
out of the way and face this man herself. He
made her *that* furious. Palmer's hand that had
stayed on her held her firm.

"It's all right, Lou," Palmer said. He tucked
his hands into his coat pockets and he rocked
back on his heels with that devil-may-care grin
he usually only trotted out when he was trying
to piss off Jack. "Ask away, bud."

There was the flicker of something in the
man's expression. No doubt irritation. No doubt
what Palmer was going for. Because Palmer
would always rather poke a bear than find a
rational, reasonable way to deal with it.

Louisa wasn't going to let that happen right
now. Not when this investigator had absolutely
no earthly reason to question *Palmer* over a fire
he had nothing to do with.

"We're not doing this here," Louisa said
firmly to Mr. Steele. "It's no place for questions, and it was highly unethical for you to
follow us here."

"Lou," Palmer said under his breath, but she
turned on him.

"No, it's ridiculous. It's freezing and we're in the middle of nowhere." She glared at the investigator. "If you want to ask him questions, we'll meet you back at Hudson Ranch."

"'We'?" the investigator repeated. As a question.

Louisa wasn't sure if anything could have angered her more. She fixed him with her best death stare. "Yeah. *We*." She whirled around and marched for Palmer's truck.

She didn't look to see if Palmer followed. Wasn't sure she'd be able to face either of them if she'd stormed off alone like a child throwing a tantrum.

But she heard the crunch of boots on snow. Palmer following her, no doubt.

Mr. Steele called out after her, "Don't worry. I'll be right behind you."

She climbed into the pickup, probably looking ridiculous avoiding the ice, and trying desperately not to think of the way Palmer had held her as he'd helped her out earlier. Because she couldn't do it *all*. Protect Palmer, and want Palmer, and hate that investigator all while her mind reeled with why any of this was happening.

She settled herself into her seat as the driver's-side door opened and Palmer hopped in, easy and graceful and with none of the scrambling she'd done.

"Should have let me help you up, Lou," he said, and it was meant to be provocative. A memory.

But she was too mad at him. "Why did you have to put on the lazy, ne'er-do-well cowboy act?" she demanded as he started his truck. "Can't you think something through for once?"

"I think plenty of things through when it comes to you, Louisa," he said, holding her angry gaze.

She couldn't tell *how* that comment was pointed, only that it was. It made her feel that obnoxious embarrassing warmth in her cheeks.

"There's no reason he should question you."

Palmer shook his head and turned his attention to pulling out of the parking lot. "He considers me a suspect."

Louisa slumped back in her seat, crossing her arms over her chest. "That's ridiculous."

"Ridiculous or not, it's what he thinks. I would have preferred answering his insulting questions on top of a mountain."

"Why? So you two could end up grappling and see who could throw the other one off the mountain?"

He shot her a quick grin. "Fantasizing about it?"

She could honestly reach over and strangle

him. "I do not understand how you can be so casual or cavalier when that man suspects you of setting a fire."

"I didn't set it. If I didn't set it, he can't find evidence to prove I did. So what's there to worry about? Why not ruffle his feathers…or grapple in a snowbank?"

She *supposed* he had a point, even if she didn't like it. She glanced in the rearview mirror as the small car followed them down the twisty roads back toward Sunrise and the Hudson Ranch. Nothing about this felt right.

"Why did he switch cars, Palmer?" she asked, leaning her forehead against the cold window. Outside, everything was white. Christmas was barreling up on them and everything was just *wrong.*

"I don't know," he said, and finally he sounded like he was taking this seriously. "Can't say as I like it, but there's this great thing about being an investigator myself. I can look into Hawk Steele, which I'm willing to bet a hundred dollars isn't his real name."

Louisa considered. She thought there was something fishy about the man, but he did seem to know Ed and have an official Bent County business card.

"I'll take that bet."

He shrugged. "Your loss, Lou." He pulled off

the highway and onto the long drive that lead up to the Hudson residence. The humor and ease that was so *Palmer* tightened into something else there on his face. He didn't look at her as he pulled to a stop in front of the house. "Maybe Anna should drive you home."

"Why on earth would I go home?"

"Why would you stay?" Now he did turn to look at her, to pin her with that dark, serious gaze that made her heart flutter. Because this was new. He never used to look at her this way. In fact, she was pretty sure he *used* to make every effort not to.

"This man is investigating a fire that happened at *my* house. I was *with you* when I got the call it happened. When your tires were slashed. If he thinks you have anything to do with it, clearly, I'm the person to prove you don't. Besides, I need to be here to make sure that you don't do your *Palmer* thing and try to make things worse for yourself."

"Is that what I do?"

"Yes, Palmer. That is what you do. Believe it or not, I get it. But *now* is not the time."

"You get it, huh?"

I get you. "Come on," she said, and she pushed her door open, hopping out onto the gravel that had been cleared of snow. Mr. Steele was already out of his car, squinting against the bright sun as he surveyed the ranch around them.

When Palmer came to meet him, Mr. Steele gave a short nod. "Some spread," he offered, eyeing the ranch with cool detachment.

"That's Wyoming for you." Palmer sighed. "Well, you both might as well come on inside. I'm sure Mary's got some coffee or hot cocoa at the ready."

Chapter Eleven

Palmer didn't often believe in being hospitable, though it was a trait his mother had held in high esteem—which again made him think of Mary, who seemed to be doing everything in her power to become a carbon copy of Mom.

So much so that if Palmer had any time to worry about someone besides Louisa, he might worry a little bit about her.

Fires came first. And Hawk Steele was part of that.

Palmer held the door open for him then stepped inside himself, putting a buffer between the man and Louisa. She seemed to think he was green enough to run his mouth to incite the investigator, and maybe he was. But he wasn't going to do anything to hurt Louisa.

Palmer pointed down the hallway and into the big living room that they often held client meetings in. "We can take a seat in here."

Palmer let the investigator lead the way then

followed so he could keep that buffer up between Mr. Steele and Louisa. Mr. Steele stopped at the entrance to the room and studied it.

"Make yourself comfortable," Palmer offered, pointing at the couch.

Mr. Steele glanced at the couch, but he didn't immediately sit. He seemed to be waiting for them to.

Palmer could play all the little power games. He was an investigator too.

Of things a lot more complex than arson.

Anna swept in, yelling at someone behind her, presumably Mary. The unreadable fire investigator stopped dead when he saw Anna. He looked at her like she was some kind of a ghost. When Palmer turned to look at his sister, her expression in return was nothing quite so shell-shocked. It was more of a smirk.

No one spoke, but there was *clearly* some kind of unsaid conversation going on between Anna and Mr. Steele.

"Do you two know each other?" Louisa asked, sounding skeptical and surprised.

Anna looked at Mr. Steele. Then at Palmer. The smirk didn't change. "You could say that."

Palmer did not groan, mostly because he knew that's what Anna expected him to do. Because it was clear, Anna had slept with the man who currently wanted to pin him for a fire he'd had nothing to do with.

Mr. Steele finally recovered, no longer looking at Anna but instead surveying the room. "Is there somewhere I can ask you questions in private, Mr. Hudson?"

"It doesn't need to be private, Mr. Steele," Louisa said firmly.

"You're not in charge of this investigation, *Miss* O'Brien."

"We can talk here," Palmer said before Louisa engaged in any more arguing with Mr. Steele. "Louisa, you should let your parents know you're here. Anna, she hasn't eaten all day."

"You don't know—"

He merely raised an eyebrow and her protest turned into a scowl. Because it didn't take being there or being particularly perceptive to know she wasn't taking care of herself.

"Oh, hell, Louisa," Anna muttered. "Come on."

"I'm fine," Louisa countered, but she let Anna lead her away with only one dirty look over her shoulder at Palmer.

He waited until he knew they were fully out of earshot and noted Mr. Steele did the same.

"Not sure we needed privacy when all you're going to do is ask me my whereabouts, probably ask about the police report the same night of the fire and, hmm, the nature of my relationship with Louisa and the O'Briens."

Steele didn't give away any reaction. He stood perfectly still, inspecting Palmer with that cool gaze.

"We can start there," he said after a long stretch of silence.

Palmer grinned, because he knew. He *knew* exactly what would be asked of him. And how little it mattered. "I was at the Lariat starting around eight the night of the fire. Then Louisa and Anna happened to come in around eight thirty or nine, I don't recall exactly. My sister, the one you seem to know, noticed my tires were low, so she mentioned it. She hadn't seen they were slashed, but I went out to leave and, once I did, and saw what had happened, I called the police."

"Your brother."

"No, I called the Sunrise Police Department nonemergency line," Palmer returned. He could try to be as cool as the man in front of him, but he'd never been any good at pretending anything except to be an exaggerated version of himself. It wasn't cool or terse or like Jack or Grant. It was smiles, charm and a total disregard for what anyone thought.

Luckily, he truly didn't care what anyone thought—so long as Steele got to work investigating the right thing. The longer this took, the longer Steele wasn't looking at the right person.

So he went through the rest of the night with the investigator. The officers who responded. Making Anna giving him a ride back and Louisa coming with them. The phone call that led him to drive her and Anna out to the O'Brien orchard.

The man took notes. When Palmer tried to get a glimpse at them, he saw they were written in some kind of precise shorthand. He couldn't explain why that irritated him, except everything about this man did.

And since he did, he decided to see if he could get under the man's frosty demeanor. "You make it a habit of sleeping with young women you don't have any business touching?"

Steele didn't so much as flinch, but the harsh line of his mouth hardened. Still, his tone was as even as it ever was as he put a careful period at the end of the incomprehensible sentence he'd just written. He raised his gaze to Palmer's. "Do you?"

"Right. The third line of questioning." Palmer tapped his temple like he was on to Steele's line of questioning, because he was. Maybe Steele was good at his job, but so was Palmer. He'd been investigating things since he'd been twelve years old. "Louisa and I have always been friends. She was practically a member of the family when her and Anna were kids. We've always been friendly, but not romantic. I suppose we've had our disagreements over the years, but nothing serious. There's yet to be any more to that story."

"Yet?"

"That's what I said. I had nothing to do with the fire, Steele, and there's no evidence to even begin to believe I did. So why don't you stop trying to wriggle me into this little problem and focus on the real problem, which is the O'Brien fire."

"I know what *all* the real problems are, thanks."

"Do they involve Anna?"

There was a flash of reaction, but it was so quickly schooled away, Palmer wondered if he'd imagined it. "What happened between me and your sister is none of your business."

"Yeah, funny. That doesn't fly for me, bud."

"I don't really care if it does."

"You don't have sisters. Do you?"

"I don't have anyone. I can tell you this. I have no doubt your sister can take care of herself *just* fine. Now, if you'll excuse me, now that I've followed this line of questioning, which was a necessary and an important part of my official, *legal* investigation, I have all those problems you mentioned to solve."

There was a slight hesitation, the briefest flicker of a glance back to where Anna and Louisa had disappeared and then almost an imperceptible shake of his head. "I'll be in touch," he muttered before stalking out of the room.

LOUISA SAT AT the Hudson dining room table, her two oldest friends watching her as she ate a sandwich Mary had insisted on making. Louisa didn't want to eat it, but she did because they were watching to make sure she chewed and swallowed every bite.

"So," Louisa said, hoping that maybe if she got them distracted, half of the sandwich would be enough to satisfy them. "Exactly how did you end up sleeping with Bent County's fire investigator?"

Mary's eyes widened and she turned to Anna, who shrugged lazily. "Well. I was over in Bent following a lead on one of my private investigation cases, stopped in at Rightful Claim for a drink. He hit on me. One thing led to another." She gave a little shrug.

"You didn't mention any hookups to me."

Anna shrugged again. "Maybe it didn't bear mentioning."

But Louisa knew her friend well enough to

know just about *everything* bore mentioning. Unless something about it had bothered her.

"He seemed pretty shocked to see you here, and that's about the only emotion I've seen on his face," Louisa said, watching Anna's carefully blanked expression.

Mary leaned over and pushed the plate closer to Louisa. On a sigh, Louisa took another bite.

"Well, we didn't exactly exchange last names, Louisa. Or details."

Mary wrinkled her nose. "Anna. Anonymous hookups. Really?"

Anna only grinned. "Have you *seen* him?"

Mary shook her head in despair, and Louisa rolled her eyes. "*You* didn't seem surprised to see *him*," Louisa pointed out.

"I'm a private investigator. Just because we didn't exchange information doesn't mean I didn't *have* information. Besides, with a name like *Hawk,* it was pretty easy to find some details." Anna grinned at her sister. *"After."*

"Heaven help me," Mary muttered. "Let's put…*that* aside. Why is he asking Palmer, of all people, questions?"

"I don't know," Louisa returned. "Palmer came over while he was talking to my parents. Mr. Steele asked if he was my boyfriend. I said no, but I think he was banking on the fire being some kind of relationship quarrel."

"I guess it makes sense," Anna said. "If he has absolutely no leads, he's got to poke into everything. Palmer's been hanging around."

As if speaking his name conjured him, Palmer walked into the dining room. Without the investigator.

"Well?" Louisa demanded.

"Well. He asked his questions. I answered them. He left." Palmer shrugged negligently. "I didn't do anything, so it hardly matters."

"But why would he even think you did?" Anna demanded.

Palmer seemed to mull this over. "I'm not sure he did. I think he's just trying to get a clear picture of all the players."

"Since when are you a player in a fire?"

"It's the tire slashing and the police report, where you and Louisa were both there, right before the fire. If he's any good, and I hope like hell he is, he's trying to find a connection."

Louisa's stomach tied into a hard knot. A *connection* between those two things could only be what she and Palmer had been investigating, and if that were true…

Louisa stood abruptly. "I should go back to my grandparents' house."

"I'll—"

"I'll take her back," Palmer interjected over

Anna's offer. "I was the one who brought her here."

"Yeah, what was that about?"

"I didn't want Agent Rabbit Rusty Iron there upsetting her family any more than he already had."

"Why were you together in the first place?"

"Because we were," Palmer said, because apparently he wanted to make this a *deal*. Likely as some sort of brotherly payback for having to know she'd slept with the fire investigator.

"You have a client coming in fifteen minutes, Anna," Mary said quietly. "You wouldn't be able to drive her anyway. And I want to go over the discrepancies in the books before you meet with him."

"Fine," Anna muttered, but she eyed Palmer then leaned forward and whispered something to him before she looked past Palmer to her. "I'm calling you later for the full story."

Louisa nodded numbly. There wasn't really a *full* story, other than the whole secret she still didn't want to let Anna in on. Especially now with so much going on. So much possibly…

It couldn't connect. *How* on earth would it connect?

With both Mary and Anna gone to deal with HSS business, Palmer turned to her. His expression was serious but unreadable.

"What did she whisper to you?" Louisa asked.

"That she was going to gut me while I slept and decorate the Christmas tree with my insides."

It surprised a laugh out of her. "Anna always is creative in her violence."

"That she is. Come on. Let's go for a walk before I drive you home."

She hesitated. Surely he just wanted to discuss the fire. Her grandfather. Hawk Steele maybe. There was nothing more to this wanting to take a walk than privacy to discuss what she didn't want anyone to overhear.

But there was *something* about the way he looked at her that was different. New. Not that it hadn't been there before, lurking in his expression at the oddest moments, but that he didn't attempt to guard it.

And how much that scared her.

"Or I can just drive you home right away, if you'd rather," he offered, like he could read her disjointed thoughts. Sense all the trepidation she had building inside her. And yet, none of that fear or concern or disquiet could outweigh what had always drawn her to him.

"No, let's walk."

She got to her feet and they walked back to the front of the house where they'd hung their coats. They bundled up and stepped outside. The sun was shining, so the afternoon held *some* miniscule warmth even in the midst of all this snow.

He led her away from the house, from all the ranch buildings. Along the fence line where evergreens were decorated with lights and natural garland no doubt Mary had made, probably with Izzy.

It was the kind of thing Louisa would have done with her mother if she'd been a little younger. If she could think of Christmas instead of all the problems around them.

"I know you don't want to upset anyone," Palmer said after they'd walked a while in silence. "I know you love your parents, but I think you need to take one of those DNA tests. And tomorrow morning, when I go talk to a few of the nurses who worked at the hospital when you were born, I think you should come with."

"If they're local…"

"I know," Palmer said gently. "Gossip is inevitable. Even if it's not, talking to people is something that could get back to your parents. I know you want to avoid that. I want to avoid it for you, Lou. But this…fires and investigators. It's dangerous. What's more important? Sparing their feelings? Or keeping you all safe?"

Both. Both were important. Both felt imperative, even though she knew safety was more important than feelings.

"Order the test," he urged. "Come with me to-morrow to talk to the nurses. I'll use my considerable charm to convince them to keep it quiet." He even grinned and winked at her, but she knew there was none of his usual ease behind it. He was trying to make her smile, and she couldn't.

"We'll have an idea once we talk to them, and if we think they can't keep quiet, we'll warn your parents ahead of time. But you have to know that's a possibility you might have to face going forward."

It sounded terrible. Except one part. "'We'?"

"You dragged me into this, Lou. You aren't kicking me back out."

Duty. That Hudson code of honor. *That's* why he was here. Not for any other reason. Except… "People are going to start talking. If they haven't already. About us spending all this time together. Particularly without Anna."

His expression didn't change, but something in his demeanor seemed to coil tight. "Yeah, they are," he agreed. With no inflection or any of his usual recklessness. This…was serious. She swallowed as he stopped their forward progress.

Louisa had been all over the Hudson property. She'd in fact spent many a summer afternoon hiding in this thatch of evergreen trees with Anna. Giggling over all the different things they'd found amusement in over the years.

There was nothing very funny about being here with Palmer. When her heart was heavy and her nerves were shot and he was so...good to her.

He took her hand. He studied her very carefully as he took a measured but deep breath. Then he pulled her closer.

And closer.

Her heart was clamoring in her chest now, and for all the different ways for over a decade she'd dreamed of Palmer Hudson pulling her close, she could not fathom how to behave in this moment. She wasn't inexperienced. She wasn't a teenager any longer. But in this moment, she felt like both—painfully unaware of *everything*.

"What are you doing?" she asked, her voice little more than a squeak when he'd pulled her close enough that their coats touched. She could feel the heat of him, and she couldn't control her breathing. She couldn't control *anything* when he looked at her with all the heat and intensity he never *once* had, even when he'd been telling her things like he didn't want to be around her.

"What I've been promising myself I wouldn't do since you came home from college."

Then his mouth was on hers. After all her years of dreaming and pining, and hating herself a little bit for the latter, Palmer Hudson was kissing her. And it was brighter, hotter and sweeter than anything she could have imagined.

Chapter Twelve

Louisa O'Brien tasted like she smelled. Of honey and summer. Her hair was silk against his cold fingertips, and their winter clothes were too bulky to really feel her body pressed against his, but it didn't matter.

She kissed like a dream he'd never allowed himself to have. Encouraging him not to bound forward in his usual reckless manner, but to slow down. To enjoy every second. Because this wasn't about chasing a feeling or finding a destination. It was just them.

She didn't touch him. And that had him pulling his mouth away, even if he still held her in place right there tucked against him. "You can tell me to stop."

Her eyes blinked open, green and magic. "Why on earth would I do that?" she asked, seeming truly confused.

It made him smile, even while something dark and a little painful twined with all this *want.* "You're a million ways too good for me, Lou."

Her eyebrows drew together. "That isn't true."

He wished he could believe that, but he knew what Sunrise thought of him. What his own siblings thought of him. Hell, what he thought of himself. Because in all his years of enjoying women, he'd never once let one matter.

Not like Louisa did.

"Everyone will think it. And be very, *very* vocal about it."

"I don't think it." She shook her head. "I don't," she repeated, reaching up to cup his face, her hands warm against his cold cheeks. Then she lifted to her tiptoes and kissed him. Like she could absolve him of all his sins by simple belief alone.

He wanted to believe she could.

There were so many things he wanted in this moment, and there were so many reasons why he couldn't have it. He sank into the kiss anyway. Louisa and the warmth two bodies could make together even in the middle of a December afternoon in the cold Wyoming landscape.

"I want you," he murmured. There was no other part of her exposed to the elements, so he had to satisfy himself by pressing kisses along her jaw.

"I guess here would be out of the question," she said on a dreamy sigh.

He laughed, though it was pained. "Yeah, it would be. Besides, your parents will worry. Maybe we shouldn't be giving Investigator Raccoon more ammunition." He eased back and smoothed his hands up and down her arms over her heavy coat. Trying to convince himself to let her go.

She studied him for a long while. He supposed he couldn't read her mind, because the stare didn't seem like regret. She *should* regret kissing him. She *should* want something better for herself.

Maybe instead of trying to tell her that, he could just try to be the kind of man who deserved her.

"This isn't just…a distraction. Is it?" she asked after a long while.

The word simply didn't make sense. "A distraction?"

"Like you feel some kind of sorry for me and thought that if you pulled out the Palmer charm—"

He was already shaking his head before she could even finish. "Do you remember one of the first nights you were home from college and you and Anna went to the Lariat?"

She seemed confused by the change of conversation, but she shrugged. "I think so. You were there. I hadn't seen you in a while."

"I was. And all I saw was this drop-dead gorgeous brunette and I wanted nothing more than to talk her into my bed—or the back of my truck, as the case may be."

Her mouth dropped open a little at that, but she didn't say anything. So he kept going, because she should know. She should be absolutely certain how this had come about.

"Then you turned around and it took my brain a few seconds to register it was you."

Her expression changed. Shuttered. "And then you didn't want to. Because I don't recall you being particularly charming that night."

"No, that was the terrible part. I still wanted to. I just knew I couldn't. So I was a jerk instead."

"I like to believe myself a great mystery," she returned, still sounding irritated. As she had been that night when he'd been so blinded by *her* that he couldn't do anything but behave badly. "But I think you know you *could* have."

"Could have talked you into bed? Sure. I think even in the deep denial I was in back then, I knew it wouldn't be that simple and easy, and that was all I was after. The ties and tangles of it all were something I thought I'd always want to avoid. I'm not the same man I was that night."

It was strange to realize how true it was. How the world had changed on him, and slowly, so slowly he hadn't fully realized it was happening, he'd changed with it.

"No." She looked up at him, *into* him maybe. "Something changed. Didn't it?"

"I don't know exactly what it was. Cash settling into the single-dad thing and Izzy becoming this…girl with thoughts and opinions. Grant coming home from war. Anna getting her private investigator's license and not *just* to make Jack mad. Mary turning into Mom before my very eyes. All these adult things going on around me because we aren't kids anymore. I guess I'd been thinking if I kept being irresponsible enough, my parents would somehow come back and knock some sense into me. But they're gone. The rest of us aren't. The rest of them figured it out before I could."

Her eyes looked watery, and he wanted to believe it was the cold and not his words that had produced that reaction. But she wrapped her arms around him and simply hugged him, and they stood there like that for he didn't know how long.

It felt strangely like saying goodbye to that old version of himself. Since he didn't want to sit in that feeling, he gave her one last squeeze then eased away. "Come on. We should get you back to your grandparents' before your parents worry."

She nodded and they trudged back through their footsteps in the snow toward Palmer's truck parked in front of the house. She held his hand, and Palmer knew if one of his siblings came across that easy show of affection he'd be hearing *all* about it.

He supposed that was inevitable now. Because he'd kissed her. Because he'd accepted he could try to be good enough for her. So there was no going back.

"You know, I was thinking…" Louisa mused. "About Mr. Steele."

"That's insulting."

She laughed. "Not *then*. Before. Because if Anna likes him, maybe he's not all bad."

"You don't know how much it pains me to say this, but I think you know as well as I do that just because she slept with him doesn't mean she *likes* him."

Louisa wrinkled her nose, but she didn't mount an argument. They got into his truck and began the drive toward her grandparents' house in Sunrise. They didn't speak much during the drive. She'd clearly already moved back to thinking about the problem at hand if she was mentioning the fire investigator. As she should. This was her life burned to the ground.

His brain was still somewhere deep inside that kiss, and everything it changed for him.

When he pulled up to the house, she didn't immediately get out. She stared at the structure with a pained expression on her face. He couldn't begin to figure out what she was thinking, so he tried to take a page out of her book and focus on the matter at hand.

"Two of the nurses live over in Hardy. I'll come by in the morning and pick you up around eight. We'll go out to breakfast. Somewhere in Hardy, make sure we're not being followed, then go talk to each of them."

She slowly turned to look at him. Whatever she was thinking was hidden very well behind direct green eyes. "Breakfast?"

"Sure. We've got to make sure we're not being followed. By Fire Investigator Blackbird or anyone else."

"Palmer..."

"I know. I know. People will talk. I'm okay with that." For the first time, it occurred to him that she didn't keep asking for *his* sake. He cleared his throat. "If you are."

"What about your family?"

He felt a stab of pain born of a lot of things. Frustration. The annoyance of dealing with Jack. But mostly, the strangely strong coil of fear that she didn't want anyone to know. "I'll handle my siblings."

"I need to talk to Anna myself. I need to..."

She shook her head. "You kissed me," she said, and it wasn't an accusation, but he didn't know what the hell it was.

"Yeah. If you had a problem with it, you probably shouldn't have kissed me back."

She shook her head again. "It's not a problem. It's just…"

He wanted to tell her to forget the whole damn thing, but she kept talking.

"My life is a mess. The biggest mess it's ever been. I hate all of this. Everything since Kyla Brown messaged me. But…" She chewed on her lip and he was almost distracted enough by that to forget the but.

But. "But?"

"You've been what I've wanted and told myself I'd never have for a very long time." She met his gaze and he saw the flicker of embarrassment there.

"Well, join the club, Lou."

She smiled a little. "I'm actually a founding member of the club going on a decade. You're relatively new in comparison."

He reached over and touched her cheek. "Long as we became members at the same time eventually, right?"

Her smile widened. "Yeah, I guess that works out."

He leaned across the console and pressed his

mouth to hers. He wanted to linger, but they were in front of her grandparents' house. People might have to get used to the fact that he was planning on kissing Louisa O'Brien whenever and however he liked, but that didn't mean he had to give anyone a show.

"I'll be back in the morning," he said.

She nodded and opened the door. "I'll be ready." She hopped out and he watched her walk up to the house before he pulled away.

He didn't feel in the least bit *ready* for anything, but that didn't matter anymore.

LOUISA FELT BATTERED by conflicting emotions. Because her life had been burned down, and Palmer had kissed her.

She'd always told herself nothing would happen with Palmer, but truth be told, she'd always wondered if they could at least have a night together. Palmer wasn't exactly picky, and like she'd told him what now felt like years ago, she knew she wasn't an ogre or anything. A night was sort of the most she'd ever hoped for.

But Palmer hadn't just kissed her. He'd told her that story about the bar when she'd come home from college. That wasn't just a talk-a-woman-into-bed situation.

She'd love nothing more to ruminate on that, *obsess* over that, but she couldn't. Because there was so much to deal with when her family had lost everything except themselves and the orchard. There were insurance questions and a million things she'd never even considered in losing everything inside her home.

She kept trying to take some of the responsibilities from her parents, but now that they'd pushed on from their shock, they seemed determined to keep her out of it. Protect her from the hard stuff.

She'd never been more frustrated by that than at this moment. She wasn't a child to be protected. She was an adult, a partner in the orchard business, and a resident of the home that had burned down.

But they shut her out—as a team—and she'd had no choice but to go to her room and try to sleep. She, of course, hadn't. She'd thought of how to get through to them. She'd thought of Palmer kissing her on a cold winter afternoon. She thought of what happened if she wasn't her parents' child, about who could have slashed Palmer's tires and set her house on fire.

She wasn't sure when her thoughts stopped whirling enough to sleep, but she didn't sleep long or well. Still, when she opened her eyes and there was a faint light coming from the curtains in the little craft room she was sleeping in, she got up, took a shower and dressed.

She considered her reflection, but there was nothing to be done. Even if she could cover up the dark circles or try to make herself look a little extra pretty for her breakfast with Palmer, pretending that it wouldn't lead to talking to nurses who'd worked at the hospital when she'd been born, all her makeup had been ruined in the fire.

Because that thought seemed especially overwhelming, she pushed out of the bathroom and headed for the usual morning sounds of her grandmother and mother in the kitchen.

She stepped into the kitchen to the smell of cinnamon rolls and her grandmother in her very normal spot at the stove. Mom was not there, which was a little odd. Hopefully she was sleeping. "Good morning, Grandma."

"Morning, cupcake." Grandma looked over her shoulder at her, then narrowed her eyes in stern consideration. "You need to eat."

Louisa pressed a hand to her stomach. Because now, on top of all the roiling stress, was the fluttering nerves of how she was going to face Palmer. Her entire future from top to bottom was a very inconvenient question mark.

Grandma tutted. "This inability to eat during tragedy must have come from your mother's side. I'm a firm believer that butter is the greatest comfort when everything falls apart. I haven't seen your mother this frail since before you were born."

Louisa frowned at her grandmother. She had a hard time imagining her mother being *frail*. "What happened before I was born?"

"All those miscarriages," Grandma said with the wave of her frosting knife. "She really had a rough go of it."

Louisa gaped at her grandmother. She had never once heard her mother even hint that she'd had a miscarriage or any sort of fertility issues. Maybe if she'd ever thought deeply about it, she'd wondered if there was something medical that had kept her mother from having a child until later in life, but she simply hadn't known enough to jump to that conclusion. "I didn't know that. Why didn't I know that?"

"Oh, I suppose your mother never was comfortable talking about it. It was a dark couple of years there. I'm not even sure I know how many babies she lost, poor thing." Grandma beamed at her. "And then there was you."

Louisa wished it could comfort her. It explained a lot about why her mother and father were so lenient with her, and she liked to think she'd been a good daughter to them. That even if they'd struggled, they'd ended up with someone who cared and was dedicated to the family and the orchard.

But in the midst of everything going on, it only seemed to point toward this meaning… She *wasn't* her mother's. That there was a very clear reason she wasn't.

"I won't force you to eat much, but I'm going to have to insist you have at least one roll," Grandma said when Louisa mechanically reached for the coffeepot.

"I'm actually going to breakfast with Palmer," Louisa said, trying to sound casual and not like her mother's sad fertility history made her want to run away. Luckily, losing everything gave her some reprieve for not acting like herself.

"Palmer Hudson," Grandma said. Her lips pursed and Louisa waited for a lecture. She almost welcomed it. It would feel normal amid all this other stuff that decidedly did not. "The Hudsons are a good family."

"They are," Louisa agreed, surprised that's where her grandma had decided to begin. She waited for a *but*.

None came.

"Handsome too. Especially the sheriff, but Palmer isn't hard on the eyes either." Grandma sent her a conspiratorially wink, shocking Louisa enough to laugh.

And, oh, she needed that laugh.

"No, he isn't."

"Still, you shouldn't drink that coffee on an empty stomach. Sit down and eat at least a half."

Louisa knew better than to argue with Grandma, so she sat and ate half a cinnamon roll, trying to listen to Grandma chatter on about church things. After a while, Louisa got the feeling Grandma was keeping her in the kitchen on purpose.

"I should probably go check on Mom and Dad. See if they need anything from town while I'm gone," she said, watching her grandmother's face carefully.

She saw nothing change there, but Grandma unerringly pointed out the window even though her gaze was in the sink washing her mixing bowl. Still, headlights and Palmer's truck were indeed on the rise in the moody winter morning. "There's Palmer now. You go on and enjoy your breakfast and I'll have them text you if they need anything."

Louisa didn't know how to argue with her grandmother, but it didn't feel right. It felt like everyone in her life was keeping a million secrets and she was the Ping-Pong ball being knocked around by them.

But she had never learned how to have conflict. It wasn't the O'Brien way, and worse, she just...hated upsetting her family. There was so much more upset to come—because no matter what was going on, someone had burned their house down on purpose.

Louisa said goodbye to her grandmother and then walked out into the frigid morning. The sun had begun to rise, but the sky was still in that winter-dawn blue stage.

She climbed into Palmer's pickup, not sure how to navigate *any* of this.

"Hi," he greeted with a smile.

He was just so handsome. It didn't change anything, or take away her bad feelings, but it soothed some of the edges enough she could smile back.

"Hi."

He immediately narrowed his eyes, studying her. "You okay?"

She'd known this about him, but she'd never had it so focused on her—that he watched people. Understood them. Often tricked them into thinking he didn't so he could make them feel better without them ever knowing he'd done it.

But he had. And on purpose.

So she ended up telling him. She went through what her grandmother had said about her mother. Explained it had always been a secret, as far as she knew.

"Well, I didn't find anything about previous health issues in my research, but I suppose I was looking at things from your birth on. I'll check into it. Maybe it'll give us some insight one way or another. But if it was really a *secret* secret, I don't think your grandmother would have mentioned it."

Louisa knew he was right and still…it sat on her heart. The knowledge. The way it connected to everything she'd started wondering. "They wouldn't have needed to steal me from *Ohio*. There would have been options," she said, not because she thought he needed to be told but because she needed to say it out loud. To reassure herself.

Palmer spared her a glance as he drove. "If there's something out of the ordinary, the medical staff would know or remember. So, we'll ask."

She was quiet the rest of the drive to Hardy. He turned on the radio and hummed to the songs that played. He didn't press for conversation or try to cheer her up, which allowed her to unwind and relax some.

He pulled into the parking lot of a diner she'd been to with Anna more times than she could count. Because they had excellent waffles, and they were her favorite breakfast food. She eyed Palmer. "Why'd you choose this place?"

He didn't look at her as he pulled into a parking place and turned off his truck. "They've got great waffles."

And she knew, the oh so *casual* way he said it, while carefully not looking at her, meant he knew. He'd brought her here because he knew she liked it.

She leaned over the center console and kissed

him. Because in all this *terrible*, he'd made something good out of it.

He pulled back from her, but he was grinning. "You're going to get me into trouble, Louisa. Shocking."

She laughed and they got out of the truck and went inside the diner. They found a booth, and he surprised her by sliding in next to her rather than across. But they didn't discuss it. They ordered their breakfasts. Palmer kept conversation light. Nothing about the fire or her parents. He talked about Mary's Christmas preparations, the annoying present he'd gotten Izzy with the express purpose of annoying the hell out of Cash, and the puppies one of Cash's dog had surprised them with.

It almost felt normal. If she swept aside everything actually happening in her life. If she somehow accepted this *thing* with Palmer was happening.

As they ate, they both glanced at the door when the little bell rang, and watched Mrs. Peabody walk in.

Louisa hadn't expected to see anyone she knew, though it was hardly a surprise. Hardy was only a twenty-minute drive from Sunrise and boasted more stores and had restaurants. Mrs. Peabody was in just about every church group with her mother, and the biggest gossip out of all of them.

And that was saying something.

The older woman immediately spotted them but didn't come over even as they finished their breakfast and asked for the check. But when the waitress came over and handed Palmer the bill, Mrs. Peabody was suddenly *there*.

"Palmer. Louisa. Good morning."

"Morning," they repeated in unison.

"How are you doing, Mrs. P.?" Palmer asked casually. His arm was resting over Louisa's shoulders, and he didn't make a move to pull it away or to put space between them like Louisa half wanted to.

"Just fine. Just fine. Good breakfast here. I won't keep you, of course, just wanted to stop by and say— she leaned forward conspiratorially "—you two make a real cute couple."

Palmer just grinned at her. "Thanks, Mrs. P."

She walked back to her booth and Louisa watched Palmer. His gaze was carefully neutral, but he quickly glanced at her to see what her reaction was.

It was kind of sweet. So she leaned her head on his shoulder for a minute. He kissed the crown of her head.

"Come on, let's get this over with."

Chapter Thirteen

Palmer drove the truck to the address he'd found for the nurse who had been on Anna's records. The plan was to start there and ask her about what staff she remembered from that year. See if there were any out-of-the-ordinary stories she remembered.

He'd considered calling the woman ahead of time, or even calling with his questions, but it was all too delicate. If there was something fishy going on, it was best to talk to someone involved in person, and without warning. That was something he'd learned working on cold cases.

Still, Mrs. Janice Menard might not be home when they got there. She might be a little leery about talking to two strangers about her job twenty-four years ago. He'd questioned a lot of people over the years, and some people *loved* to talk. While some people had watched too many cop shows and insisted on getting a lawyer first.

You never knew what kind of person you were going to get. For Louisa's sake, Palmer hoped Janice Menard was easy.

Luckily, they hadn't suddenly developed a tail. Hopefully that meant Hawk Steele was off looking for the actual arsonist this morning. Palmer didn't trust the man, but everything he'd dug up on him pointed to a brilliant investigator who went above and beyond. If there were secrets in Hawk's past, or an identity with a normal name, Palmer had yet to find it.

So he hoped that it was all true. Hawk Steele was a great investigator who would find the perpetrator so Louisa's family could have some closure.

And stayed the hell away from Anna while he did it.

Palmer drove into a nice little subdivision not far from the hospital. According to his research, Janice Menard had retired two years ago. He hadn't been able to find any information on her husband, but he'd been more focused on getting the information on the nurses as individuals. Then, if anything popped out, he'd dig more into their families.

He pulled to a stop in front of the address. The house was nice and well kept. Christmas lights wound up around the pillars in front of the door, and snowmen grinned from the windows.

There was a large Christmas-themed wreath on the front door and little toy soldiers lining the walk up to it.

Palmer turned to study Louisa. He liked to think breakfast had distracted her for a bit. He knew it wouldn't last forever, but his heart twisted at the sight of her pale and studying the house like it had all the answers she wanted. And didn't.

She wanted the truth, and didn't, and if there was a complicated emotion he understood above all else—it was that. Because sure, he wished he knew what had happened to his parents, but at the same time…those details couldn't be pleasant or comforting, particularly all these years later.

So, he understood what she was going through. Better than most.

"We'll just ask her a few questions then go from there. Let me do most of the talking, but if you think of something you want to ask, go on and ask it."

Louisa didn't look at him, but she nodded as a sign she was listening.

"Lou…"

She finally looked at him and he reached over and fitted his palm to her cheek. "I know it all sucks. No one's expecting you to feel good about this, but I promise you, we're going to do everything we can to get to the bottom of it. Not just the truth, but the fire too. We'll get you answers."

"Thanks," she said. She didn't look any more comforted.

It ate away at him, but he also knew there were some situations a person just couldn't find comfort in.

He got out of the truck and took her hand when he came around to her side. They walked up to the front door together. Palmer dropped her hand when he knocked on the door, because he wanted to create a professional image when he talked to the former nurse.

A woman who appeared to be in her sixties, fitting the description of Janice Menard, answered after a few seconds and looked at both of them with a polite smile, but eyes full of wariness. "Hello. Can I help you?"

"Hi, my name's Palmer Hudson. I'm a cold case investigator with Hudson Sibling Solutions." He held out one of his business cards that Mary had made for them all to add "legitimacy" to questioning people. He almost never used them but figured this was one of those situations it might ease some of that wariness.

The woman took the card with wide eyes. She studied it then looked back up at him. "What's this about?"

"I'm investigating a cold case. We're talking to nurses who worked at St. Mary's Hospital here in Hardy in the late 90s and early 2000s. That's how we came across you."

"Oh, well. I'm not sure how I could have been involved in a cold case. I was a labor and delivery nurse." She pocketed Palmer's card.

"We just want to ask some questions. If you don't remember, you don't remember. But we're looking into a situation that might have been a little out of the ordinary. Like a newborn being placed with a family that wasn't theirs. Biologically."

Janice's forehead creased and she seemed to give this some thought. "That seems like something I'd remember, doesn't it? I was a nurse for over thirty years, and lots of things just blur together," she laughed. "But I think I'd remember a situation like that."

Palmer nodded kindly. "We just had to ask. Do you remember anyone you worked with maybe discussing a situation like that? Maybe not even specifically. Just something that felt off."

Again, Janice seemed to consider this. "Well," she said, eyeing Palmer then Louisa. "Now that you mention it… I'm not sure this is what you're looking for, but I do remember a little hubbub about…" She wrinkled her nose. "I don't remember the details, or maybe I never poked around for them. But definitely something hush-hush about a newborn, and it wasn't that I heard specifics, more hints of gossip. It was supposed to be a secret, but one of my good friends was the nurse. She didn't tell me anything except... Well, there had been a very odd situation, and if I'm remembering it right, it's right in your time frame."

Palmer glanced at Louisa, who'd somehow gone even paler. "Do you remember the name of the nurse?" he asked, reaching out and taking Louisa's hand.

Janice definitely studied the move, but Palmer found he didn't care when it looked like Louisa had been stabbed.

"Oh, sure. Birdie. Birdie Williams. We were the best of friends. We still keep in touch. Would it help if I gave you her address?"

"It would, Mrs. Menard. It sure would."

"I'll be right on back." She turned and disappeared back into the house, though she left the door open a crack.

Palmer gave Louisa's hand a little squeeze. "It doesn't mean anything just yet. Something to look into."

Louisa nodded but didn't say anything. He could see her mind had zoomed into a million different possibilities, but he'd investigated enough cold cases to know it was just as likely a dead end as anything else.

Janice returned with a little piece of paper. "Off Rural Route 2." She smiled and handed it to him. "I hope this helps you get the answers you're looking for."

"Thank you, Mrs. Menard. We sure do appreciate it. And if you think of anything else, call my cell. It's on the business card."

"Of course." She moved to close the door but Palmer held up a hand.

"I just have one more question, if you don't mind?"

"Oh, of course not." Her smile stayed in place but she still held the door half closed. Hard to blame her when they were strangers, he supposed. But still… There was something that didn't sit right, and he didn't know what it was just yet.

"What brought you to Hardy? You're one of the few nurses I found on the roster who wasn't from Wyoming."

She smiled even wider. "Family."

LOUISA FOLLOWED PALMER back to his truck feeling numb, and it had nothing to do with the cold. This felt like a lead and she…didn't want a lead. She wanted to go home and bury her head in the sand.

Except her home had burned down, and something worse might happen if she didn't figure out why.

They got into the pickup and Palmer began driving again, but instead of two hands on the wheel, he put one over hers. "We just have to take it one step at a time."

She swallowed at the lump sitting in her throat. "Yeah, I know."

He drove and he kept his hand on hers, but she noticed that he wasn't exactly the same as he'd been after the diner. He seemed more alert. He was constantly looking in the rearview mirror, like he was waiting for someone to pop up out of the woodwork.

"What's bothering you?" she asked when he frowned even deeper as the GPS instructed him to turn onto a gravel road.

"I did a basic profile of Janice Menard. I don't recall seeing any family in the area. That's why I asked why she moved here."

"Maybe she meant extended family?"

"Could be. Or even her husband's family. This just feels… Can you look on your phone and see if you can find any pictures of this house she's sending us to?"

"Do you think she was lying?" Louisa asked, sitting straighter in her seat, her heart rate starting to pick up.

"I don't know. Just got a bad feeling about something."

She scrambled to get her phone out and typed in the address on the piece of paper while Palmer took another turn, this time onto a dirt road. She began to feel some concern too. This was way outside of Hardy. Deserted.

It did not feel right.

But she found a couple listings, with pictures of the house associated with the address.

"It looks like your typical old ranch house," she explained. "Maybe a little run-down, but this says it was built in 1920, so that makes sense. Especially if an older couple lives there."

"Birdie Williams is on my list of people to talk to, so it's not like Janice made her up. I'll look at my notes before we head in there, but if I'm remembering correctly, she retired five-ish years ago when her husband passed away. So, she's likely living there alone, unless there's family with her."

Louisa studied him for a minute. "You don't need to look at your notes, do you?"

"Huh?"

"You remember it all. Exactly as you said. You don't need to look at your notes. You're just trying to look like… I don't know. I don't understand why you go through such lengths to let people think the worst of you, Palmer."

And she didn't know why she was bringing it up *now*, but it was just so incongruous.

He was helping her. He was practically the only thing keeping her together the past few days. Yet he still had to downplay what he was capable of. It didn't make any sense.

She loved him—and not even in that same way she'd thought she'd loved him at thirteen. This was deeper. More meaningful. *This* was an adult feeling, because she was an adult and she understood so much about him now.

But she didn't understand this.

"You don't understand because you don't have older siblings," Palmer replied. He wasn't trying to make a joke of it exactly. He was more making light of it. "Especially ones who are saintly sheriffs and war heroes."

She frowned. "So instead of, say, being proud of them, and confident in your own abilities and choices, you have to pretend to be the family clown and act like you don't care about anything?" Honestly, men really were the most infuriating creatures.

"You'd have to have siblings to understand," he repeated. He glanced at her with a kind of rueful smile before looking back at the road. This one was no longer plowed, so Palmer had to slow the truck to be able to determine where the road was and drive it safely.

"But I get your meaning, and you're right," he said. "I am proud of them, and I don't have regrets about the choices I've made, so there's no real reason to feel like I have to act down to less. It's a hard habit to break because that's how we work. The Hudsons and HSS are a well-oiled machine, and we all have our roles."

"I don't think you being who you are is going to somehow mess up how your family or business works, Palmer."

This time when he looked at her, he really smiled. "As I hear tell, I don't need any help with my ego, Lou."

"Yes, well, I think it depends on what ego we're talking about." She wanted to say something else, but she didn't know what. Just that she appreciated all that he'd done, and she wanted him to get the credit he deserved for it.

Palmer let out a low whistle as he slowed to a stop at the directive of the GPS. "Either the GPS is wrong or Mrs. Menard is." He inched forward in the snow, closer to the dilapidated house, squinting as he studied it.

"I think it's the same house in the pictures," Louisa said, looking at her phone then back up again. "I just think these pictures might be ten years old." The house wasn't just run-down now, it was clearly abandoned. She *hoped* it was abandoned. The ceiling was caving in, windows were broken, gutters hung off the roof. There was a barn next to it in even worse shape.

"It might appear abandoned, but look." He pointed out past the house. She squinted at the blinding white and didn't see anything.

"Tracks," he explained. "Some footprints, some snowmobile. Even if it *looks* abandoned, someone's been out here." He scanned the scene in front of them, and Louisa did the same.

She wanted answers to her life, but… "Palmer, I don't like this."

"Yeah, me either. Let's go. I'll do some research on Birdie Williams and we'll go from there."

Louisa nodded. She still looked around the house and the barn, trying to discern why it felt so disquieting. There were plenty of abandoned and falling-apart ranch buildings in this area, but this one felt…wrong.

"Can't go any farther forward or I'll get stuck in that bank," Palmer said. "Have to reverse and try to turn around." But before he could back out, she saw the flash of movement in the house.

Just as Palmer jerked her down and something around them exploded.

Chapter Fourteen

There was only one gunshot. It had shattered his windshield, which was far too close for anyone's comfort. Palmer covered Louisa's body with his the best he could in the cramped front of the pickup.

They were sitting ducks, even with the protection of the truck. "Stay down. I'm going to try to drive us out of here."

"But—"

"Louisa. Keep your damn head down and don't *move*."

She didn't pose an argument this time and Palmer moved, keeping his own head and body down as best he could, but putting himself in a position that allowed him to gauge things a little better.

"Call the police. Text my family. Whatever you can do on your phone without moving."

He jerked the truck into Reverse, angling his body so he could see out the side-view mirror.

If he wasn't careful, he'd just reverse them into being stuck in the snow.

"I don't have any service," Louisa said.

"Of course not," he muttered. He carefully eased his foot onto the gas, pulling away from the house, still waiting for another shot to go off. It didn't, but he could hardly be grateful when he couldn't see beyond what he could make out from the side-view mirror.

He was so focused on reversing that it took him a minute or two to realize something was wrong. Even more wrong than just the situation.

He smelled…gas.

He shoved the truck into Park. "Out!" He reached over and undid her seat belt for her, then practically dragged her across the console. He didn't even think about gunshots at this point because he knew that if that first bullet had done the wrong kind of damage, the truck could very well explode. Regardless of whether they were in it or not.

Louisa didn't mount an argument or struggle against him as he pulled her from the pickup, or if she did, he was too focused on getting her to safety to notice it.

"Run," he said once they were both free of the truck and on their own two feet. He kept her hand in his as he started running. He pulled her in a kind of zigzag pattern just in case whoever had fired was waiting.

The sound of the truck exploding echoed through the quiet winter morning. He pulled Louisa down behind a snowdrift. The snow wasn't any kind of protection from whoever was out there with a gun, but it kept them out of sight from anyone in that house or barn.

He peeked over the snowbank at his truck. Now on fire. "Someone's really got something against my truck."

"Palmer…"

"It's all right. We'll be all right." He didn't know what the hell was going on, but he'd do everything in his power to make sure Louisa was all right.

"I know you're going to want to argue with me. But I need you to do what I say, exactly as I say."

"I'm not leaving you," she said firmly. Because she clearly saw where he was going with that.

It was the only way. "Lou." He swore inwardly at the stubborn lift of her chin but couldn't let it stop him. "I know how to handle this. We can't get help without some kind of cell service. I've got a gun. So you run toward where we came from. You should be able to get service not too far back."

"Would you leave me?"

He wanted to tear out his hair. "We do not have time for this. Someone shot at us and *some-*

one needs to be the one to get help. It's my gun. I know how to shoot it. So it doesn't matter what I'd do, this is what we have to do."

"Palmer—"

"Damn it all, Lou—"

"No, Palmer. Look." She was tugging on his arm and he finally looked over to where she was pointing. There was a man walking toward them. With a gun.

Luckily, Palmer had his own gun on him, had in fact been wearing it since he'd left the house this morning. He moved to remove it from his holster. He kept his eyes on the approaching man but reached for Louisa.

"Go. Now. I can handle this but only if you go get some backup."

He crouched behind the snowbank, making sure his body would be between Louisa and the gunman no matter what she decided to do. "You're going to run, staying low and zigzagging. Back toward where we came from. Find cover. Use your phone. Be smart. Someone starts shooting, you run harder. You hear me?"

"All right," she said. "But I'm coming right back. The minute I have service and get through to someone. I'm coming right back."

He didn't have time to argue with her. The gunman was somewhere behind the blaze that engulfed his truck. He held his gun at the ready, watching for him to come around either side. "Just go."

So she did. He heard her quiet footfalls but didn't dare look back at her. She was smart. She was capable. And he hoped to God whoever she got to come out and help them told her to stay put.

When the man with the gun still didn't appear from either side of the fire, long after the sound of Louisa's escape had faded, Palmer took a split second to glance over his shoulder.

He saw Louisa dart behind a tree then back out. Following instructions. *Thank God.* He wasn't sure how far she'd need to go to get service, but it didn't matter. There was something to deal with here.

He crouched as low as he could and still move, practically crawling behind the swell of snow that had been made by gusts of wind. He wanted to take the shooter off guard if he could.

But when he stilled, looked over the snow again, he could tell the shooter knew exactly what his new position was.

"Was it really necessary to ruin my truck?" he called out. He didn't expect an answer, but maybe there'd be some clue as to who or what he was dealing with.

Unfortunately, he couldn't think of a way this didn't connect to Louisa digging into her true parentage possibility. Janice Menard had sent them here—and the woman *had* been a nurse at the hospital. It wasn't just a strange coincidence.

Palmer started moving again, wondering if there was any way he caught this gunman off guard. He hated the idea of shooting first and asking questions later, but then again, this guy wasn't exactly asking questions.

So, Palmer decided to throw out a few more of his own. "I don't suppose we could clear this whole thing up with a conversation?" After he spoke, he quickly moved in the opposite direction he'd originally been moving.

Nothing but silence.

"Because I don't have a clue as to why you're beating up my truck." He thought about bringing up the fire at the orchard, but Louisa hadn't fully understood him when she'd accused him of playing dumb.

He did do what she said. Play down to expectations and act like he couldn't quite hack whatever was going on around him. He liked to, sometimes. Because it made people underestimate him.

When it came to investigating, sometimes that worked in his favor.

"I don't really want to shoot you," Palmer called out again. He knew the guy was creeping ever closer. In his mind, Palmer picked a spot that would be his last straw before he pulled his own trigger. "But I'm also planning to see Christmas, so it's going to be an inevitability if you don't stop where you are."

Palmer was surprised when the man actually stopped, though he still didn't say anything. He didn't move. He stood on one side of the snowbank and Palmer crouched on the other side. Seconds turned to minutes, and minutes stretched out. Until Palmer thought his toes, fingers and nose had gone completely numb.

He couldn't stand like this forever. He'd given Louisa enough time to get hold of someone—God, he hoped. He very carefully and quietly curled his finger around the trigger of his gun.

Before he could decide on his next step, the gunman's cell phone chimed. The man touched something in his ear. Listened and then touched it again.

Palmer heard something else...like a...scream? He scanned the surroundings, looking for Louisa, gunman forgotten until the man spoke.

"Bad news, bud. We don't need you," the man said, and then, before Palmer could fully dive out of the way or lift his own gun, pulled the trigger.

LOUISA WORKED IT out so that she zigzag ran for a count of thirty, then checked her phone. If she didn't have service, she ran for another thirty seconds. It killed her to have left Palmer, but he was smart and strong and… He could handle this. She had to believe he could handle this.

Because if he couldn't, it would be all her fault. Clearly, this all connected and, if she'd only kept it to herself, it wouldn't have gotten so out of hand. If she'd ignored that Facebook message, everything would be *fine*.

Her lungs were burning and there was a sharp pain in her side, but she didn't let up. When a bar of service finally popped up on her phone screen, she nearly wept with relief, but she didn't have time for that. She found a tree to huddle behind. It wasn't great cover, but it would have to do.

She wanted to call Anna or even Jack, but the smart thing to do was to call the emergency line at Bent County, where someone had to pick up no matter what. She squeezed her eyes shut as the phone rang.

"Bent County Emergency Line. What's your emergency?"

"We need help." Louisa didn't bother to explain what kind. She just rattled off the address. "Send someone quickly. There's a gunman and a fire and…just send somebody." Because she needed to get back to Palmer.

"Ma'am. Slow down. Give me more details."

"I don't have any. There's a man with a gun.

He shot our truck. We need help. Now!" She didn't end the call. She couldn't stay on it either. Maybe it was foolish, but she left the phone there, resting on top of the snow. If someone needed to ping it, they could, here where she still had service. If she needed a phone later, Palmer had one.

Because this was the last time she was going to separate from him as long as someone was trying to hurt them. He would not take the brunt of this. She couldn't let him.

She ran back toward the house. She couldn't even begin to guess how far the distance was. She could see Palmer's truck smoking, though most of the flames had died out by now. She could tell Palmer was still huddled behind the snowbank, but she was still so far away.

She didn't zigzag this time. She needed to get to him as quickly as possible. So she could...? She didn't know. He was the one with the gun. Was she really expecting to run in and save him? She'd likely get herself, *and Palmer*, shot.

She slowed her pace. She couldn't make out the gunman's face from this far away, but she didn't think he was paying attention to her. Just yet. Maybe if she rerouted, she could come up behind him. Surprise him.

She couldn't hear anything other than her ragged breaths and the howling frigid wind. She needed to get hold of her breathing, carefully sneak around, and maybe the wind could help disguise her approach.

Louisa came to a full stop, planning to look around to find the perfect route. Before she could, someone grabbed her from behind, pulled her back hard.

She tried to yell, but a hand slapped over her mouth so that it was just a muffled sound. She tried to fight off the strong arms that had banded around her, but the grip was tight. She was dragged backward a few steps as she fought to free herself.

She thought she was succeeding, or at least keeping the person from dragging her any farther, but then something was being put over her head.

She screamed this time, because there was no longer a hand over her mouth, but whatever was over her face muffled the sound as well. She couldn't see now. She could only fight her unknown attacker as she was hauled through the snow.

She kept fighting. Kicking out and jerking her arms as best she could. Whoever had her—however many of them there were—they were too strong. Whatever was on her head made it hard to breathe, impossible to know where anyone was.

She kept trying to scream, but inhaling a deep breath only pulled the material over her face into her mouth. Which caused terrible bolts of panic to beat through her. She had to fight them off—panic, the people. She had to get to Palmer.

Whoever had her was dragging her, so she decided to suddenly go limp. It seemed to take them off guard enough that someone lost their grip and she fell into the snow. She immediately tried to get to her feet, to roll away and throw out some punches, but the grapple in the snow only lasted a moment or two before she was lifted up.

Clearly, there were two people involved— someone carried her by her arms and someone by her legs, as she tried to jerk and bend her body in whatever ways she could to get them to drop her again.

Instead, she was given a kind of toss and shove, and she landed hard...*hard* against a ground. Not the snow this time. Were they inside? The house maybe? Or the barn?

Something exploded from not far off. A gunshot. Louisa stilled without thinking the thought through, listening hard for some kind of reaction to that shot. Was it Palmer shooting? The gunman shooting Palmer? Something else?

But there was only the sound of the howling wind, a thud, then an engine starting and something that sounded like...a van door rolling closed.

Her hands were pulled roughly back but she tried to wriggle away—to keep kicking and fighting and not choke out the sobs that had welled inside her. Had someone been shot? Was Palmer okay?

How was either of them going to get out of this?

Her hands and legs were quickly secured. She could only roll now, and she felt the rumble and acceleration of a vehicle. She was in a car of some kind, not a house or the barn. They were driving away with her tied up and some kind of hood fitted over her head.

Louisa tried not to panic. Desperately tried to keep her breathing even so she didn't suffocate in the material. She couldn't fight them off. She was in this vehicle now, so she stilled. She tried to count her breaths in and out.

And think. *Think*.

Surely Palmer was okay. Surely help was on its way. This was scary, but…it wouldn't end badly.

It couldn't.

Then she listened to what the voices were saying.

"Not dead yet, but he'll bleed out before anyone finds him," a man said.

Louisa made a shocked sound of pain, because there could only be one *he* in this scenario.

Palmer.

Chapter Fifteen

Palmer had never been shot before. For a moment, he could only sit there somewhere between realization and pain. He looked down at the sudden river of blood pouring out of his side and wondered how this had all come to be.

Focus, some inner voice warned him. He looked from the wound to the gunman. Even raised his own weapon to belatedly defend himself, but the man was running away. Toward the barn. Or something behind the barn. Palmer couldn't tell from his vantage point.

Well, at least the guy hadn't finished him off.

Palmer looked back down at the bullet hole in his side.

Probably hadn't finished him off anyway.

He realized dully he was in shock. And the fact that he wasn't screaming from pain just yet couldn't be good.

None of this was good.

But Louisa was out there. Getting help. She

had to be. She'd probably do something ridiculous like come running back here and blame herself. She'd probably even cry over the whole thing. He sucked in a painful breath and forced his gaze away from the blood. He squinted into the snowy world around him.

He just had to wait it out. She'd be back and... it'd be okay.

Unless that strange noise had been her. Because the gunman had taken a phone call, so he wasn't acting alone. Had someone gotten to her? Hurt her? He didn't see her anywhere, and she should be visible, shouldn't she?

That thought pierced the weird fuzziness around him. They couldn't get their hands on Louisa. They couldn't hurt Louisa. He had to save her.

He tried to get up, but nearly passed out instead. *There* was the pain. He tried to tell himself that was a good thing as his vision blurred, threatened to go gray. It meant his body wasn't giving up just yet.

He'd been shot. He had to think. What was he supposed to do?

Save Louisa.

He shook that thought away. He would do that, yes, but first he had to make sure he didn't bleed out. He had to find a way to *get* to her without just crumpling.

He needed to put pressure on the wound. Stop

the bleeding. It couldn't be good to lose this much blood, even if he was still breathing and mostly coherent.

How was he going to stop the bleeding out here in all this snow, his truck blown to hell? The only thing he could think to do was to pull off his gloves, ball them up and shove them against his torn, bloody shirt.

The sound that came out of him as he did this was somewhere closer to animal than human, but he knew well enough that no matter how badly it hurt, he had to press harder to stop that tide of blood.

He breathed through that for a few seconds. Fought off the creeping blackness. He wouldn't give in to that. Not until he knew Louisa was okay.

Once he thought he could bear it, he tried to stand again, but he just couldn't move that way without such excruciating pain that his muscles wouldn't work. Everything gave out, and he was breathing so hard he thought he might throw up. He was lucky he didn't collapse in a heap.

Okay, so standing was out. But he had to move. He'd crawl, roll. Whatever he had to do to find Louisa.

He managed to get to his knees, one hand still pushing the gloves into his side and the other balancing himself upright on the ground. His vision swam and everything threatened to just give in and give out.

He had to find Louisa.

He sucked in a breath and let it out. He pushed in on the damn bloody wound and let himself make whatever terrible noises he needed to make to get through it.

Why had the gunman run off? Left him here to...

Well, die.

No. He wasn't going out that easy. Not when Louisa might be in trouble. He couldn't leave her to the wolves. Something had to be done.

He wasn't able to stand. Not the way he was feeling. He wasn't steady enough, and a fall could send him over the edge. But he could move forward on his knees.

Or so he told himself. But moving was becoming increasingly difficult. His limbs felt heavy, and a numbness was spreading through every last inch of him. It was hard to focus. He just kept repeating Louisa's name—out loud, in his head. Whatever it took to focus on what was important rather than the pain. The fear. The fog trying to overtake his mind.

Eventually, he sensed movement. He was able to turn his head enough to see a car. With flashing lights. Followed by an ambulance. Both sped through the snowy street with more urgency than caution.

The cop car skidded to a stop and Jack was out of the driver's side before it had even fully stopped skidding. Deputy Brink got out of the passenger side, just a few steps behind Jack.

Who was shouting? Palmer tried to make sense of the words before he realized Jack was yelling at the guys in the ambulance.

Jack knelt next to him, reaching out to steady Palmer's wavering frame.

"What the hell happened?" he demanded, his hand coming over Palmer's and the wadded-up gloves trying to soak up the blood.

Jack pushed even harder, creating more pressure on the wound and more pain arcing through him. Palmer hissed out a breath.

There was so much to explain to Jack, but none of it mattered until they figured out where Louisa was. "I can't find Lou. She was with me then she called for help. But she hasn't come back. I don't know where she went. We've got to find her."

Jack and Deputy Brink exchanged a look. Deputy Brink immediately walked away, and Palmer could hear her ordering people around, though he couldn't make sense of what she said.

"Palmer. What *happened*?" Jack demanded, crouching just out of the way while the medics worked in tandem to examine his wound and get him on a stretcher.

Palmer did his best to explain it to Jack—all of it. From Janice Menard to this moment right here. He wanted to keep Louisa's secrets, but he needed her safe more than that.

He could tell from Jack's frustrated expression—and lack of more questions—that whatever he'd *thought* he'd been saying didn't make much sense.

"Tell Anna to go through my files," Palmer said, wincing as the medics started to move him. "She can hack into them no doubt. She'll figure out specifics. Janice Menard. Janice and… Jack, where is Louisa?"

Because if Louisa was okay, she would have come running once she saw the cops and the ambulance. She would be there. And she wasn't.

Jack said nothing. He looked over somewhere in the distance, but he did not answer Palmer's desperate question.

"Jack, where the hell is Louisa?" he yelled at his brother as the medics put him into the back of the ambulance.

We'll find her were Jack's terse words as the door closed, separating them.

Palmer was left with the medics and his own fading vision.

He had to stay awake. He had to help…but

before he could even attempt to fight off the medics, his world went dark.

LOUISA HAD STOPPED putting up a fight. There was no point to it. Something tied her wrists and ankles together. If she got too worked up, she couldn't breathe well enough in this hood thing. She was clearly in a moving vehicle, so nothing could really be done in the moment.

She couldn't fight her way out—not yet—so she had to be smart. She had to listen and think and plan.

She could not dwell on the fact that the gunman thought Palmer would bleed out all by himself. She'd called for help. Someone would help him. He'd be okay and then he'd find her.

She knew he would.

So she had to stay alive. And get to the bottom of this the best she could so that when Palmer got her out of this, they'd have all the answers and be able to put all this…sheer insanity to rest.

Palmer couldn't die. It was just…impossible.

Well, Jack surely wouldn't allow it. She tried to convince herself of that. Jack Hudson was too rigid, too demanding, too perfect to ever let his brother die.

Tears came and went. She'd get a grip on them, then they'd threaten again, but if this hood got any damper, she'd struggle even more to breathe. She needed to keep it together from here on out.

It felt like they'd been driving forever. The people in the vehicle didn't talk. So far, only the man who'd spoken of bleeding out—the gunman she'd seen—had said anything. She tried to recall details of the man. He'd been average height and build. Nothing special about him, but he'd had a beard. Darker, maybe a little gray, so not a young man. She hadn't seen his eyes or anything distinguishing, but he'd been wearing tactical pants and a black heavy coat and hat.

She would get out of this and she would make sure everyone responsible was held accountable for their role in…whatever this was. So she would remember every last detail she could to repeat to police once she was saved.

Louisa held on to the belief she'd be saved.

She tried to determine how many people were involved right now. The man who'd shot Palmer. Someone driving the vehicle. There had to be at least one other person because two people had thrown her in. So, three people minimum.

They'd shot Palmer, left him to *bleed out* and taken her. Very much alive.

And that Janice woman had sent them here. She had to have known. It had to have been a setup. So, at least four people were involved.

How many others? Why?

It had to tie to Kyla Brown's message. There was no other logical explanation. Not that fires and shootings were *logical*. But she'd stumbled into something bigger than just…whatever she'd thought it was.

Louisa kept going over the information in her head, trying to commit every detail to memory. Trying to keep herself from thinking about Palmer and bleeding out and how damn scared she was of where these people were taking her and why they were taking her alive.

There was no way of knowing how much time had passed when the vehicle finally began to slow. The people around her didn't speak. Not as it stopped. Not as doors opened.

Roughly jerked out, she was placed on her feet and her ties were cut. Someone held one elbow, while someone else held the other.

"Walk," the gunman's voice ordered.

She hesitated, because she wasn't ever keen on taking orders, even when she was scared to death, but that was the wrong move, apparently. The man squeezed her arm so hard, she yelped in pain.

"I said *walk*," he ordered.

Her feet began to move before she'd fully thought the motion through. She didn't want to follow his orders, but her arm screamed in pain. Walking made him stop hurting her, so she walked.

The hands on each arm led her in the direction she needed to go. The hood felt more and more suffocating until Louisa thought she was going to pass out. But she couldn't. She had to be alert for everything.

Because she *would* get out of this, and when she *did*, she would remember everything. And all of these people would pay.

They had to pay.

She was shoved and thought she would fall since she couldn't see, but her butt landed on a hard surface, arms still holding her even as her body jolted with the impact. It was a hard chair she'd been pushed onto. Her arms—already tied behind her back—were suddenly wrenched and she realized they were now also tying her to the chair.

She didn't cry, though it was a hard-won thing. She breathed. Carefully. Focusing on her breaths over anything else. If she panicked, she wouldn't survive. So she couldn't panic.

She had to *think*.

With no warning, the hood was removed. The world around her wasn't bright, but Louisa still had to blink a few times going from fully dark to a dimly lit room.

Room might be generous. It was more like a... cellar. The ground was packed dirt, the walls were made of rocks. It was clearly some kind of old, deserted building that, at some point, a few people had converted into some kind of shelter.

She didn't see any supplies, just three people in this strange little space that smelled of earth and cold.

Louisa looked around. There was the gunman who'd presumably shot Palmer. She'd been right about the gray in the beard. His eyes were dark, and he had a scar across his chin. There was the hint of a tattoo peeking up from his collar.

She turned her attention to the two other people—both women, both young. One was dressed casually. Jeans, a hoodie, even average tennis shoes. Her hair was hidden in a knitted winter hat, but her eyes were blue. The only thing intimidating about the woman was the large and very dangerous-looking gun she held.

The other woman…looked familiar. Similar, even, to Louisa's own reflection. Dark hair, freckles over her nose. Her eyes were brown instead of green but…

And that's when Louisa realized. "Kyla?" The woman who'd messaged her. The woman who'd started this whole thing.

"Heya, sis." The woman smiled, as if they were meeting in a coffee shop, not with Louisa bound to a chair in a creepy old cellar. "Nice to meet you in the flesh."

Sis.

Louisa swallowed. "What…is happening?"

Kyla Brown stood by a small window. She was dressed in all black winter gear, and it looked vaguely tactical. Lots of pockets and hooks and things. Her hair was pulled back in a severe French braid. Her gaze was narrowed on that window that seemed to look out only into snow.

"That *is* an interesting question," Kyla said, as if mulling it over. As if this was a normal conversation and not kidnapping and attempted murder.

Attempted, because Palmer had to be okay. He *had* to be.

"These damn snowstorms have really messed with my timeline. If that wasn't bad enough, *you* and your boyfriend had to go poking around." Kyla sighed and shook her head as if despairing of them. "Oh, well, it'll be a nice Christmas gift."

Louisa wanted to believe this could be fixed. That everything could be okay, but there was something about the *casualness* in Kyla's tone with all these guns and bad things…that told Louisa this would not be okay. Very, *very* not okay. "What will be a nice gift?"

"You, of course." Kyla turned to face Louisa and her pleasant smile made Louisa's stomach sink and turn. Nothing about this should be pleasant. "It's time *everyone* pay," Kyla said. "And you're the key."

Chapter Sixteen

Palmer woke up in a hospital bed. He knew right away they'd pumped him full of something. He felt foggy and heavy. Thoughts wouldn't coalesce the way they needed to. Because he needed to do something. What was it?

He looked around the room, blinking away blurry vision. For a split second, he thought the woman sitting in the chair next to his bed was his mother. His heart leaped.

Then broke.

"Mary."

Her head shot up, like maybe she'd been nodding off sitting there. She hopped up and immediately her hand was on his face. "You are in *so* much trouble," she scolded, her voice a croak, like she was trying to hold back tears.

"I don't remember…" But he did. He'd been shot. He knew exactly where he'd been and what he'd been doing. He tried to sit up. "Lou?"

Mary's expression didn't change, but something in her eyes flickered as she pressed him back into the hospital bed. "You have to rest. You were *shot*. You lost a lot of blood. You've been in and out since they stitched you all up. They think you'll be able to go home tomorrow if you can walk around a bit, but you have to take it easy." She blew out a breath and studied him, clearly struggling with a lot of emotions she didn't want to let loose.

She hadn't answered the one thing he needed to know. "Mary." He fixed her with his sternest stare in his currently fuzzy state. "Where is Louisa?"

Mary inhaled. She tried to smile, but he knew his sister too well. It was only bad news.

"They're still looking for her," she said, clearly trying to sound chipper and failing spectacularly. "Everyone is looking. Jack, Grant, Cash, Anna. Everyone's out there. They'll bring her home."

"How long?"

"Palmer, the situation is being handled. Now, you were shot. Seriously. Just because they think you might be able to come home tomorrow doesn't mean it was a flesh wound. There will be a long period of recovery. So you need to rest. To take care of—"

"If you think I'm going to rest while you avoid all my questions, you're not as smart as everyone always gives you credit for. How long has Louisa been out there? How long have they been looking for her?" he demanded. He looked around for a clock but didn't see one.

He couldn't remember everything. His memory of the morning was kind of foggy, but he'd been with Louisa. He didn't know what time it had been, or what time it was now, but he remembered being shot and not being able to find her.

Now Mary was being far too quiet. "Damn it, Mary, how long?"

"It's been about twelve hours since you were shot." She sighed when he tried to sit again. "You are hooked up to an IV. You've been *shot*. Stop trying to be a superhero and think rationally."

"Think rationally? She's been missing for twelve hours. That means someone *took* her. She didn't wander off. She didn't get lost." He struggled to breathe past all the terrible possibilities. "She could be hurt. She could be—"

"We're not thinking about what she *could* be, Palmer," Mary said firmly. Not that *I'm-in-charge* kind of firm he was used to from her. There was something vulnerable about how forcefully she'd said those words.

She swallowed. Hard. "We're focusing on the facts. The facts are Jack and his department, along with us, and Bent County, and half the town are out looking for her. So we won't deal in abstracts. We will deal in facts."

Facts. The fact was Louisa was *missing*. She needed help. Because if she didn't, she would have made her way home. People wouldn't need to search for her. Louisa could handle herself, so if she hadn't come home on her own, she was…

Mary squeezed his hand. "If we think of all the possibilities, we fall apart. We can't fall apart. You need to rest. You need to get better. And you need to let everyone who's able to handle finding her. Okay?"

"How do you expect me to just lay here? *I* know what's going on. *I* was there."

"And you were shot in the process. You aren't any good to anyone if you're dead. If Louisa hadn't called emergency services, you would be. You *would* be." This time tears glistened in her eyes. "I don't know why you and Grant had to decide to be bullet magnets this year, but it's going to have to stop."

It was the tears that got him. Even though it felt like he couldn't breathe, even though Louisa was out there…with someone. Hurt or not, she was being held against her will. Still, he tried to smile reassuringly at his sister. "Thick skin. We're okay."

She shook her head. "But you could have not been."

He squeezed the hand she held. "I thought we weren't dealing in abstracts and coulds?"

She let out a little huff of irritation, and still she didn't cry. Because they'd been through too much. They'd learned how to carry too much on their shoulders.

But he couldn't bear this. "You gotta get me out, Mary. I can't just stay here. I have to find her."

"Do you think Jack or Anna or any of them are going to rest without finding her?" Mary demanded. Her voice faltered, but she didn't drop his gaze or his hand. "You have to do what's best for yourself and for Louisa. You charging out there and then passing out because you lost too much blood is not what's best for anyone. You will stay put. And you will rest."

Palmer opened his mouth to argue, but a tear slipped over and onto her cheek, so he shut it. She was upset, and he couldn't…push her. Mary didn't cry. Even when they'd been kids, she'd tried not to cry. When Anna threw tantrums or raged over a boy—complete with tears and swears and the occasional breaking of things— Mary had held it all together.

"Okay," he said to keep her from crying—not because he planned to do it. He'd just need to figure a way to outmaneuver her. "Why don't you go on home? Get some rest yourself."

Mary's eyes narrowed. "Do you really think I'm a fool?"

"What? You're going to spend the night here? In this cramped uncomfortable hospital room? I'm sure I can charm the nurse into taking care of me just fine."

"I'm sure you can charm the nurse into all manner of things I wouldn't approve of. So I'll be staying put." She reached over his bed and hit the button that would call the nurses' station.

Palmer wouldn't be deterred. One way or another, he was getting out of this hospital bed, and he was going to find Louisa and bring her home.

LOUISA COULDN'T REMEMBER ever being so cold. Her three captors had built a small campfire outside the structure's walls and took turns going to warm themselves by it. Inside the little cellar building, small battery-powered lanterns offered light to see by, but absolutely no warmth. Louisa shivered and struggled to move her fingers or her feet, or anything that might help warm them up.

No one spoke around her, so she still had no idea what was going on. Sometimes she could hear muffled voices outside when they were all out there, but nothing was ever clear enough to catch.

It was very careful and purposeful, which was both frustrating and terrifying. Whatever this was, it had been planned. That meant it would be harder to find the means to escape.

She had to escape. She just had to. Someone would come help her. She believed that too, but if she could get herself out of this, then there was less chance of anyone else getting hurt.

She swallowed at the lump in her throat because Palmer could be dead right now. All because of her.

Louisa looked at Kyla, who stood in her spot by the window. Even though it was pitch-black outside, she kept her gaze there. She would stand for what felt like hours, unmoving, just holding on to a gun and staring blankly out the window.

"Kyla?" Louisa ventured. When the woman looked over at her, Louisa tried to smile. "Can you tell me what happened to my friend? The one that guy shot?" She didn't want an answer, but... How could she not ask?

Kyla shrugged and looked back out the window. "It doesn't matter."

"Well, it does to me. I..." Why did she feel compelled to tell her kidnapper she loved

Palmer? It hardly mattered in the here and now. But him being okay mattered. "I need to know."

Kyla shook her head. "You better be careful or you'll end up just like her."

"Like who?"

"Our mother." Kyla looked back at her and considered. "I hate to break it to you, but all she ever cared about was men. She was unfaithful to my dad, and that made you. That's why…" She narrowed her eyes at Louisa and took a few steps toward her. Louisa had to work hard not to instinctively pull away.

Kyla crouched in front of her. "I know you want the truth, and I want to give it to you. We're sisters." She smiled kindly. It died quickly. "But I also gotta be real careful. I have a plan. If I don't stick to the plan, things are going to go bad."

Louisa swallowed. "I just don't understand because I thought… I thought you wanted to be sisters. Family. I don't have siblings here. You don't have any back home, do you?"

Kyla shrugged and rocked back on her heels. "Depends on how you look at it. Like I said, our mother is a real problem."

Our mother. Louisa tried not to focus too much on that. Just because this woman said it was true didn't make it true.

But she saw herself in the woman. The *girl*.

Louisa knew she was only nineteen. What was she doing with guns and plans that involved kidnapping?

"Maybe if you told me the plan, I could help."

Kyla stood to her full height, looking down at Louisa with a sneer. "Don't do that. You think I'm that gullible?"

"Of course not." Louisa tried to keep her expression neutral. "Kyla, I am freezing. This isn't good. None of this is good, but it could be okay. You can't keep me here. I'll die."

Kyla moved back over to the window. She didn't say anything.

"Kyla?"

Still no response.

Louisa sucked in a breath, held it for a few counts, then let it out. She had to think clearly. She couldn't cry. She couldn't panic.

She was alive, and that meant everything was within her reach. Palmer was okay because she'd called for help. She would just...believe it. There was no point in imagining he was dead. She might as well give up then.

And she wouldn't. She was going to figure a way out of this.

This woman was supposedly her sister, surely there was some way to appeal to that fact. She thought of how Mary or Anna would treat a sibling in this situation. Differently—Anna would yell, Mary would persuade, but they'd both be firm and clear.

"If I don't get food or water or warmth soon, I'm not going to make it," Louisa said firmly. "If that's the plan, fair enough. But if you want me alive, I need help. I'm *freezing*."

There was a moment where Louisa thought it wouldn't get through to Kyla. That she would keep standing there staring out the window with absolutely no response.

Louisa tried to think of a new approach, but Kyla moved. She said nothing, offered no explanation, but she left the cellar building.

When she returned, it was with a mug. Steam curled in wisps, indicating something hot was inside. Louisa nearly lost her battle with tears. She was so beyond hungry, she felt vaguely nauseous, but more than anything, she was so very cold. Something hot would… It would give her strength. Hope.

She was in desperate need of both.

"I'll untie you so you can eat this but understand that I'm going to shoot you if you try anything. Okay?"

Louisa nodded.

"I don't want to, but no one is messing up my plan."

Louisa nodded again. "I understand."

Kyla set the mug down on the floor and then

moved behind Louisa. After a little bit of fiddling, Louisa's wrists were freed. This time tears did trip over and onto her cheeks, even though it made her even colder. But her arms ached—moving them was agonizing and yet the position she'd been in was painful too.

Kyla came back around to the front of her and looked at her disdainfully. "You're going to have to toughen up, sis. It's going to be a while yet. I've got a plan, but if your people track us down, I'm not afraid to start shooting."

She picked up the mug and handed it to Louisa. Louisa's ankles were still tied together and to the chair, so there wasn't really any chance of her escaping anyway. She one hundred percent believed Kyla would start shooting if she even *thought* Louisa was making a run for it.

She'd have to find a smart way to escape. Right now that meant eating the soup. It hurt to hold the mug, but Louisa wasn't about to drop the first touch of warmth she'd had in hours. For a few minutes, she simply cradled the mug.

Unfortunately, that gave her time to think. It looked like your typical canned soup, but what if it was something else? What if it was poisoned? What if *that* was the plan?

"I'm not standing here watching you forever. Once I'm ready to go outside, the mug goes with me. Eat or don't, but you better do it fast."

Louisa swallowed. Well, if it was poisoned...
Maybe that was better than starving to death.
Or being shot. She brought the mug to her lips
and sipped the soup. If nothing else, it tasted as
soup should taste.

And it was warm. Hot, even. It took every last
ounce of strength not to start sobbing. She had
to stay strong somehow though. So she slowly
and methodically drank the soup. She didn't
try to talk or move or anything. She kept her
brain as blank as she could. All she focused on
was the soup.

Once she was done, she tried to draw out the
moment. Just holding on to the mug, taking a
few fake sips from it. Because she knew the moment she stopped, Kyla would want to tie her
back up again. The cold would return.

Kyla wasn't fooled for long. She moved forward and tried to take the mug. Louisa knew it
wasn't smart, but she held tighter to the mug.
Desperate for this connection to something
warm.

Kyla jerked it hard, so Louisa lost her grip.
She would have toppled forward, chair and all,
but Kyla used her body to keep Louisa upright.
Then she set down the mug and went to work
tying Louisa up.

Louisa didn't fight it. What was the point?
She was certain Kyla would shoot her if she

tried to run. For whatever nonsensical reason, she'd been taken and kept alive…but there had to be a *reason*.

"It's freezing in here when I can't move or do anything," Louisa said, trying to appeal to *some* humanity within the woman who now stood before her again. The woman who was supposed to be her sister.

Kyla studied her. Louisa couldn't read this stranger's expression. Clearly, everything was off about her. She wasn't behaving rationally, so there wasn't much point in trying to rationalize her behavior.

Then she simply walked out of the building, leaving Louisa alone again. Louisa squeezed her eyes shut, counting her breaths. If she was alone, she had time to consider her escape. If she was alone, she wasn't being hurt. Alone was good.

But it was so unbearably cold.

After a few moments of Louisa doing everything she could to keep her mind off the cold, Kyla returned, a folded blanket in her hands. Carefully, almost reverently, Kyla wrapped the blanket around Louisa's tied-up body. The girl's brown eyes studied Louisa. Then she shook her head, almost sadly.

"I'm sorry it can't be different," she said. "But it's all our mother's fault." Kyla shook her head again. "And she has to pay. You understand that, don't you?"

Louisa swallowed and held Kyla's gaze. Maybe she couldn't rationalize anyone's behavior, but she wanted to understand. She wanted to make sense of this in any way she could. So she worked on sounding agreeable. Understanding. "I want to, I do. But I'm not there yet."

Kyla reached over and patted Louisa's head. "Don't worry. Once they get here, you'll understand everything." She let out a long sigh. "It's just a shame that then you'll have to die."

Chapter Seventeen

Palmer hadn't been able to outsmart Mary, though he'd tried all through the night. He'd even once managed to take the IV tube out, capped off the needle in his arm and made it all the way to the end of the hall.

A nurse had stopped him, because somehow even all his charm couldn't get through to her. Because Mary had gotten to her first.

The nurse had threatened to call security. Palmer wasn't above fighting off security, but he'd been struggling to stay upright so he hadn't liked his chances.

The nurse escorted him back to his room and reattached his IV. Mary had woken up in the time he'd been gone, and she looked furious. She had a phone to her ear, so she didn't start yelling at him while the nurse took his vitals for the five hundredth time.

"I believe I just proved I can walk around fine. Shouldn't that mean y'all can let me out?"

"That's up to the doctor, Mr. Hudson."

He smiled at the nurse even though he didn't feel like smiling. Or doing anything other than fighting someone. Not that he had the energy left in him to fight.

Once the nurse left, he turned to Mary. He already knew there was no new news or she would have immediately told him. Still, he had to ask. "Anything?"

Mary pursed her lips. She didn't meet his gaze. "They've got search parties. The police are on the lookout for Janice Menard. Cash has the search dogs out as much as possible."

"Not very helpful in the snow."

"No, it isn't, but he's trying. Everyone is trying."

He knew she was right. Rationally, he even knew him being out there looking wouldn't change anything, but just sitting here was like having needles shoved into every inch of him. It wasn't the pain from the gunshot. It was an emotional pain. A feeling of helplessness that he had worked so very hard to never have to feel again after his parents' disappearance.

And failed. When Grant went off to war. When Anna had insisted on rodeoing and getting herself hurt. When Louisa's house had burned down and he hadn't had any answers for her.

He couldn't just *sit* in these feelings. It was unbearable. "Couldn't you at least bring me my computer?"

"No. Because you are supposed to rest. You also need to stop refusing your medication."

"I'm not in that much pain." The physical pain had nothing on the twisting feeling inside his chest that Louisa might be hurt. Or worse.

Mary only gave him a look. Then she seemed to remember her phone in her hand and shoved it in her pocket. "Anna and I are going to switch off." Mary looked concerned about this. "Jack said the only way he could convince her to leave the search party was to put her on Palmer babysitting duty. She's running on fumes. So, I'll take her place, and that means you need to stay put so *she* stays put. Got it?"

As if on cue, the door opened and Anna stepped inside. She had dark circles under her eyes and a kind of grimness he remembered from those first days after their parents had gone missing. A grimness that hadn't belonged on an eight-year-old.

Still, there it was. All these years later. With more people they loved missing. Eight, twelve, twenty-four, twenty-eight, it didn't matter. It felt awful.

Mary looked from Anna to him and shook her head. "I don't trust either one of you."

"It's almost like you know us," Palmer offered, hoping to get a smile out of Anna.

Her expression didn't change. Palmer didn't know how to lie there and pretend it would all be okay if Anna didn't.

Mary rolled her eyes and crossed over to Anna. "Honey, I think you should go home for a few hours. Rest. I can stay here and—"

"If you're taking my place, you should go. We need all hands on deck." Anna swallowed. "It's already been too long. We can't let it go any longer." She didn't meet eyes with either Mary or Palmer.

Mary nodded then gave Anna a hug that Anna didn't return. "Be good, you two. *Please*." Mary waited a beat, looking at Anna and then Palmer, then sighed and shook her head.

No doubt knowing that they would absolutely not be *good*. How could they be? Louisa was out there and they were not sit-and-wait type people. Never had been.

Anna stared at him. "I got into your computer and Dahlia went through all your notes. She caught us all up as best she could. We still don't have any idea who took her, but the thought is it has to connect what you guys have been researching."

"Connect any dots?"

Anna shook her head. "Last I checked with

Dahlia, not really. Probably need your computer expertise, though Dahlia is doing her best. They even brought Hawk up to speed, hoping something in the arson investigation connected, but they haven't found anything yet." She sucked in a breath. "Why didn't Louisa tell *me*? Ask for *my* help?" Anna asked, her voice rough from lack of sleep. "Why did she trust *you* with this?"

"We can go through all that," Palmer said, struggling to keep his voice even, "as soon as you help get me out of here. I've *got* to get out there."

Anna looked at him and the hospital bed. She was already shaking her head before she even spoke. "Palmer, you were shot. They said you could have died—"

"Yeah, Mary mentioned. Over and over again. That was yesterday. This is today. I'm fine. Or fine enough anyway. I cannot lay here while Louisa is missing, in trouble, possibly hurt. I can't. If you don't help me, I'll do it on my own. Eventually, I'll get past somebody and do it on my own."

"Why do you care so much?"

A sharp pain sliced right under his heart—again not physical. Nothing painkillers would help with. For so many different reasons, he couldn't meet Anna's sharp gaze. "You know why."

"Yeah, but I want to hear you say it."

"Fine." He glared at her, because leading with anger made more sense than feeling any of the terrible things rumbling around inside him. "You'll be the first. I'm in love with her, okay?"

Anna nodded, and she looked like she was about to cry. But she just blinked a few times and cleared her throat. "Yeah. Okay. I've got your computer in my truck. You can look up whatever you need to while we drive."

"Where are we driving to?"

Anna shook her head. "Hell if I know, but we're not going to stop until we find her."

LOUISA WOKE WITH a start. She realized dimly her arms were no longer tied behind her back, though she didn't remember being unbound.

Had she been saved? Her eyes flew open and she looked around desperately. She was still in the cellar building, and it was daylight now. She was cold, but not as freezing as she'd been last night.

She was alone, and her wrists weren't bound together. She didn't want to get out from under the warm blanket, but maybe this was her chance. The door that had been open last night to the fire outside was now closed. Maybe it was locked or chained and that was why they'd untied her.

It didn't matter. She'd find a way to escape. She'd do whatever it took. She kept the blanket wrapped around her as best she could, sat up and began to try to untie the ropes around her ankles.

Everything hurt. Her vision swam. She was starving and cold and a million bad things. But the thought of escape fueled her. She *knew* people were looking for her. Maybe it had been an awful long time and no one had showed up, but she knew she couldn't just disappear into thin air.

Too many people loved her, and that was a bit overwhelming in the moment. Emotions battered her—likely from the lack of basic necessities that would have kept her mind sharper. She blinked the tears out of her eyes and focused on getting the ties off of her.

Everything hurt, but the pain all kind of melded together like a dull ache. She tried to jump to her feet and immediately regretted it— her legs nearly giving out. A quick and lucky wave of her arm found the wall and she was able to lean against it to fall with less impact than she might have without it to help her.

Louisa sucked in a breath and worked on sitting first, leaning against the wall, pulling the blanket back around her. There couldn't be any panicking. She had to be smart and careful.

This time when she got to her feet, she took it slow. She used the wall for balance and gave her legs the time they needed to have her blood circulating again. She didn't think she was actually injured anywhere, just stiff and dehydrated.

If she could get outside, at the very least she could get some snow. She had no idea how long it had been since Kyla had brought her soup, but if her stomach was anything to go by, it had been a while.

Still using the wall as leverage, she made her way over to the window Kyla liked to stare out of. There was no actual glass in the window. It was just an opening. So much colder over here by the window. It was big enough, she could definitely crawl out of it if she had to, but the problem would be leveraging herself that high.

Louisa reached up, wincing at the twinge in her shoulder, but ignoring the pain as she tested whether there was any way to pull herself up or to jump up or—

"What did I tell you about trying to escape?"

Louisa whirled around to see Kyla standing in the doorway with her arms crossed over her chest. The gun was on a holster at her hip now, and Louisa felt slightly emboldened by the fact that Kyla didn't pull it out and point it.

"You told me I have to die," Louisa said. Maybe she should be soft and biddable, but she just…couldn't take it anymore. "You think I'm just going to sit here and *take it*?"

"You don't understand," Kyla said petulantly. "Our mother has to pay, and you're the only way I can make that happen. Better to be dead than like her, let me tell you."

"I can assure you, I don't agree. No matter what or who she is. I'd rather be alive. Wouldn't you?"

Kyla shook her head. "No. Never."

Louisa almost felt a twinge of pity for the girl. "Surely you don't mean that. I mean you get to choose. It's your life."

"My life?"

That was *clearly* the wrong thing to say.

Kyla's eyes practically blazed with fury. "*My* life? My whole life has been about *you*. About poor lost Colleen. Mom expected me to do everything because Colleen wasn't around to do it. No one could upset Mom because Colleen had been kidnapped! She was probably dead, but no one ever knew for sure. You got to be a picture on the news and all I ever was, was an *afterthought*. A problem."

"I'm…sorry, Kyla. I am sorry that that happened to you. I don't think it was my fault. Or your—our—mother's." It was impossible to think of a stranger from the news articles as her mother. Impossible even now to believe her mother had been part of some kidnapping scheme.

How could it be true? How could she believe this young woman with a gun and an unhinged plan was somehow telling more truth than Minnie O'Brien?

"You don't think. But you don't know, Colleen. You weren't there, so you don't know anything." She shook her head, like a dog shaking water of its fur. "Not the plan. This isn't the plan. Why aren't you tied up?"

"I'm cold and hurting and starving. You can't just…keep me here and treat me like… This is worse than someone would treat an animal, Kyla. You have to at least give me some heat, some food and water, some—"

"Somehow I'm not surprised you've turned this around and made it all about you," Kyla returned.

If Kyla didn't have a gun, if even a second of this made sense, Louisa might laugh, because it wasn't all that different than how Anna and Mary had talked to each other when they'd been younger and arguing about something.

Louisa looked at Kyla. They looked so much alike. They had to be related in some way. There was just no way they weren't.

Could she really believe she was this woman's sister?

"Sit back down on that chair," Kyla ordered. She reached for her gun.

Louisa looked at the chair and then, probably ill-advisedly, shook her head. "I can't. I'm sorry. I am. But you can't tie me up again. I can't take it."

Kyla scowled but she didn't pull the gun fully out of the holster. "I clearly can't trust you to just stay put."

"No, fair enough. But maybe…maybe you could give me a reason to stay put. I know it's not the plan, but plans have to be flexible, right? If I understand why this is happening, or what you're trying to do, maybe I could agree to be tied up again."

"I could just shoot you."

Louisa swallowed and kept her gaze on Kyla's. Imploring. Hopeful. "You could. But if we really are sisters, couldn't you just let me in instead?"

"We aren't full sisters, you know," Kyla replied, not as if she was imparting new information or even a secret, but as if that made her better somehow.

Louisa was having a hard time keeping up. "We aren't?"

"No. See, I thought if I could find out who took you, I could fix everything. Mom would be good to me. If I could get you back, then we could be a happy family. Dad would stop hitting everyone, and they could stay married. Then it wouldn't be about poor Colleen. About Mom. It could be about *me*."

"That's too much of a burden on one little girl," Louisa said, feeling some strange twisted compassion for her captor.

"It was," Kyla agreed, nodding emphatically. "But I was going to make it okay. Imagine my surprise when I found out that my mother was a lying *slut*. All those stories about a kidnapped sister were faked."

Fake. That didn't make any sense. "But I saw the stories. I… It was in the news. You said so yourself. Not fake."

"She *paid* someone to take you. So my dad wouldn't find out."

"That's absurd."

"You'd think, wouldn't you? But it isn't. It's true. I have all the proof. I found all the proof, and then I knew she needed to pay. She's on her way, and she's going to *pay*. She wanted to protect you, but she can't. She won't."

Louisa stood there and knew…no matter what parts of this story were true or fake, there was no getting out of this alive if she went along with Kyla's plan. Maybe someone would find them. Or maybe Palmer had died and no one had any clue where she was.

Maybe there was only her to save herself. It didn't matter either way because it was clear Kyla was not of sound mind. There was no reasoning with her, no getting to the bottom of things.

There was only escape.

Maybe it was the absolute wrong thing to do. Foolish and reckless and every rash thing. But she pulled back her arm and punched Kyla in the face as hard as she possibly could.

Kyla's head snapped back, but she didn't go down. She started to reach for her gun, so Louisa did too. If she could get control of the gun...

Anything was possible.

Chapter Eighteen

Anna drove—though Palmer wasn't convinced her sleep-deprived state was any better than his shot-yesterday state. At least *he* could keep his eyes open.

"Search warrant finally came through right before I got to the hospital," Anna said, catching him up to speed on everything that had happened that Mary either hadn't known or hadn't seen fit to tell him. "Jack sent Chloe and a team in to do the search. He's still out in the field with the search team, the O'Briens and some volunteer groups. They followed some vehicle tracks for a bit, but the snow and the dark made it hard to do much with it. Daylight should help, and as we hit twenty-four hours, the FBI will get involved soon."

Palmer typed away on his computer, trying not to think about *twenty-four hours*. It had taken more time than he'd like to set up his hotspot, and now he was combing through anything he had on Janice Menard and Birdie Williams. Addresses, prior residences, owned properties. Anything that might give him a clue into where someone might have taken Louisa.

"You should probably yank that," Anna said, jerking her chin toward the capped IV needle in his arm.

"Aren't you going to do it for me?"

She scowled at the road. If they had nothing else, they had this. They both knew the other didn't like needles. They could handle guns, being shot apparently, forcing their body beyond the limits of what it should do—both in the rodeo and as investigators—but the whole *needle* situation made them both a little squirmy.

If he thought about that—Anna's weaknesses, the needle—he wouldn't think about Louisa. About all those possibilities that could have happened in the past nearly twenty-four hours.

Because Mary had been right yesterday. They had to deal in facts, not in maybes. The fact was he didn't know where Louisa was. He could think of a million outcomes, but he didn't know which one was close to being correct. So. Present. Not future. Not past.

Just right here, finding the answers to get to her.

"It all begins with that Janice Menard. Someone set that fire at the O'Brien house, but it didn't hurt anyone. Louisa wasn't even home. Whatever that was, it wasn't the same as Janice sending Lou and me to that abandoned house. She sent us there knowing we'd be hurt."

Palmer typed and stared and tried not to get frustrated. Dahlia had compiled a tidy list of properties owned by Janice Menard and Birdie Williams. The address they'd been sent to had been owned by Birdie Williams but, according to Anna, the questioning of Birdie hadn't led anywhere helpful.

Also, according to Anna, police and search parties had already exhausted any and all other properties owned by either woman.

There was no sign of Louisa.

"If I take you to the original site, one of Jack's deputies is going to tell Jack. We have to be careful about where we go look if you're going to be in on it. I wouldn't put it past him to throw you in a cell if he thought it'd keep you staying put."

Palmer nodded. He'd known as much. "Just drive *toward* the Williamses' property. Maybe I'll come up with a new direction to take," he said, gesturing at his computer.

He was the computer expert. So there had to be something he could find. Some clue. Some possibility. Louisa couldn't disappear into thin air like his parents had. She just...couldn't.

He wouldn't survive it again.

Anna's phone rang and she answered it over the Bluetooth in her truck. "What do you have for us, Dahlia?" she asked.

"I found something," Dahlia was saying over the speaker. "It might be nothing, an odd co-incidence, but it's worth noting. I've already told Jack, but I knew you two would want to know too. Janice Menard has a connection to the Brown family. The one that messaged Louisa over Facebook."

Palmer went very still. "What kind of connection?" he said, trying not to bark it out like an order. Dahlia might be dating his brother, but she wasn't a Hudson. He could hardly bark orders at the sweet librarian.

Even if he wanted to in the moment.

"It's very tenuous, but Janice's ex-husband, Pat Menard, is from Lakely, Ohio. Since that's where the Browns are from, I started digging. He's the cousin of the mother of the woman who sent that Facebook message to Louisa. It's kind of a roundabout tie, but I don't think we can overlook any kind of connection at the moment."

"No, we can't," Anna agreed. "Any other leads about where Louisa might actually be?"

"No, but I've started looking into property records for not just Janice's ex-husband but also *his* family in Lakely. If there's anything in Wyoming, I'll send it to everyone. I figured if you broke Palmer out of the hospital, you've got his computer and he can probably do it faster and more thoroughly than I can."

"How do you know I broke him out of the hospital and we're not just sitting here playing checkers?" Anna returned.

"Uh-huh," came Dahlia's reply.

Palmer was barely listening. He was tracking down Pat Menard and his family in Lakely. Finding anything he could. Because it had to connect.

It just had to.

"I'm going to have to stop for gas before we get any farther out of town," Anna said after she'd hung up with Dahlia. "Maybe you can find something by the time I'm finished."

Palmer grunted in assent. He focused all his attention on his computer. On finding anything about Janice's ex. Pat Menard and Janice had divorced some three years ago, and Pat had moved to Las Vegas.

Palmer found a previous marriage for Pat, which included two adult children living in the Lakely area. Palmer had started doing some digging into both of them when he heard Anna talking.

Not to him.

He looked up from his computer and saw Anna standing there, driver's-side door open. She'd clearly already gotten gas, but she was glaring at a man.

Hawk Steele.

"What are you doing here?" she demanded.

"Likely the same thing you are," he replied. "They let me take a look around the property where Palmer was shot. I found some of the same accelerant in the barn that was used in the O'Brien fire. It all connects, so I'm investigating. I think I've got a lead."

"Does it have to do with Janice's ex-husband?" Palmer asked.

Palmer noted a small flicker of surprise on Hawk's face before it went back to being unreadable.

"Yeah, it does. Janice's stepson owns some property about fifteen miles away from the Williamses' residence. It's just property. Far as I can tell—"

Palmer was already typing away. He found it before Hawk got the sentence out. "Off Rural Route 7. No house. No buildings. Just property, and it doesn't look like he does anything with it."

Palmer looked up at Hawk, who was frowning. "No evidence of anything but a holding."

"Did you tell Jack?"

"Not yet. Just got the information myself.

Was fueling up and figured I'd check it out myself rather than take the search party away from the area we know for sure she was in."

Anna looked over at him and Palmer considered. They needed all hands on deck, but his brother would likely cuff him and have a deputy send him back to the hospital.

But it couldn't just be the three of them, no matter how much he trusted Anna and himself. They needed everyone.

"Give him a call. Don't tell him you told us though. We'll have maybe a bit of a head start before he sends some people over, but it doesn't matter. All that matters is finding Louisa."

Hawk nodded, eyeing Anna and then Palmer. "Neither of you are in any shape to drive. Hop in the back, Blondie. I'll take it from here."

Palmer reached over the console hoping to stop his sister from her inevitably punching Hawk in the face. His hiss of pain as the move hurt his side distracted and kept Anna from her anger, he hoped.

Palmer wasn't sure if Hawk was that foolish or didn't give Anna enough credit for actually doing it, but neither mattered right now. "I'll get in the back," he said.

Because all that mattered was getting to Louisa.

Louisa didn't get a hold of the gun, but she did manage to knock it away from Kyla. She had two choices, and there was no time to decide which one was best. Instinct took over.

She ran.

The door had been left open and maybe she should have kept making a play for the gun but getting out and getting away just seemed far more important. Or maybe, if she were being honest with herself, she just knew she wouldn't be able to shoot Kyla, so escape was really her only option here.

She ran. Out into the cold morning. The snow made it hard to pick up speed, but as she looked around at her surroundings, she saw rocks and trees and far more possibilities for hiding places than there had been back at the original location.

There was still a campfire, but no one else seemed to be around. Or if they were, they were hidden. Louisa also didn't see any vehicles, though she did see vehicle tracks.

"Don't make me shoot you!" Kyla shouted from behind.

Louisa didn't even bother to look back. She just ran as fast as she could through the snow toward cover.

A gunshot went off, and an involuntary noise erupted from Louisa. A little gasp or scream of shock and fear. She didn't stop running. Because nothing hurt. It had sounded close, but no bullet had hit her.

She made it behind a boulder. She crouched so her head was hidden and didn't stop moving. Her eyes darted around her surroundings, constantly looking for shelter but knowing there was no stopping. As long as she was moving, she was less of a target and maybe she could find help.

She didn't really know if Kyla would kill her, and that was the problem. There was no way to predict how this was going to go. All she could do was run.

Which was also a gamble. In a Wyoming winter when she didn't know where she was. But someone would find her. Too many people would have to be looking for her not to find her.

So, she ran. She crouched behind boulders, darted behind trees, and though she occasionally heard Kyla yell something at her or scream in frustration, there was enough distance, enough natural elements, to hide behind so that she felt almost safe.

The sun was out in force, shining down on the snow making the world around her blinding. And showing her tracks all too well, but she didn't have time to cover them.

She didn't have *time*. She tried to fight off the panic, but she heard a man's voice in the distance. And not one that made her think she'd been rescued. She was almost certain it was the man who'd shot Palmer.

It wasn't just Kyla looking for her now.

She had to do something. She took a brief moment to stop, to look around. If she started climbing those rocks, she could get up off of the snow. Maybe hide her tracks a little better. If she could scramble high enough on that mountain, she could see farther. Get an idea of where she was. Maybe spot help.

It was risky, because she wasn't quite as steady on her feet as she usually was, thanks to lack of food and water, but she couldn't think of any better plan.

She started to climb. She didn't know where Kyla or the man were in relation to her position, so it was hard to maneuver herself in a way she thought would keep her hidden, but she did her best.

Her limbs were shaking. She wouldn't get much farther without risking a fall. She paused, trying to take in her surroundings. Trying to get an idea of what direction she needed to go in, or how she might signal to someone—someone who would help her, not shoot at her—where she was.

She wasn't high enough. All she saw was rock and a little bit of the place she'd come from. She also didn't spot any of her captors, which she supposed was good.

She had to climb higher, no matter how shaky she felt. She turned back to the rocks. They were getting bigger, so hard to get around and up. But it was her only choice. Her only shot at freedom.

So she reached and climbed, pushing her body way beyond its limits.

"Because I'm going to get out of this," she whispered to herself, a quiet motivation. "I am strong enough to endure this. I have to get home. For my parents. For my grandparents. For myself. For Anna. For… Palmer." She wanted to cry, thinking about the fact that Palmer might not be okay, but she didn't have *time*.

A gunshot went off again, and it startled Louisa enough that her foot slipped, her ankle gave out and she tumbled to the hard, rocky ground. Pain shot up her ankle. She barely swallowed a yelp and moan of pain. She breathed through it as her vision swam, as she tried to take stock.

It was twisted, yes, and she'd landed on a rock so now her side ached. She hadn't hit her head though or anything else, so that was good. Even better, there were very few tracks here since the snow only piled up in dips and crevices, so they'd have a harder time finding her.

That gunshot had been farther away, so she had time. She just had to *think*. She tried to get to her feet, but the pain in her ankle was so excruciating, she nearly yelped and fell all over again.

Okay, running wasn't going to work, she thought, on her hands and knees, breathing heavily. She could still hide. On her own terms. She looked around. Where there were rocks and mountains, there had to be caves.

She saw an opening not too far off. It was *really* small, and she didn't *love* enclosed spaces, but it was better than sitting out in the open waiting to be found and shot.

She crawled, trying desperately not to sob in pain. Trying to ignore the hard ground, or the cold snow she had to crawl through, making her pants and sleeves wet.

Louisa didn't whisper anything to herself now. She just focused on that cave and did everything in her power to get there. To pretzel herself into the dark, enclosed space that made her want to scream in panic.

She huddled in on herself. Now cold and wet and hurt. It was better than being a prisoner. Anything was better than that.

She held on to that belief, and then tried to come up with a plan on how to get out of this.

Chapter Nineteen

Palmer didn't pay much attention to the drive. After he'd offered to get in the back, Anna had grumbled at him to stay put and she got in the back and let Hawk drive. Palmer focused on his computer, on this property.

He looked at the map, tried to memorize it. "There's no real road in, according to the map," he explained to Hawk as Hawk drove down the highway. "You'll get on the rural route and then we'll have to trust the GPS coordinates to get us to the right place to hike in."

Palmer hacked into some satellite imaging and considered. "It looks like there's some kind of structure on the southwest end. Not a house, but definitely a building of some kind. Or what was once a building."

"We'll get close to that spot then," Hawk said, turning off the highway and onto the rural route.

Palmer looked out his window for a minute.

She had to be out there somewhere. This had to be the lead they needed it to be. It *had* to be.

"They would have wanted some shelter overnight," Hawk mused. "Especially with a captive. A building—even a structure of some kind that allowed shelter—wosuld be helpful."

"Unless they were prepared to camp and hide in the mountains. Or, you know, you're leading us on a wild-goose chase," Anna said from the back.

Palmer spared her a glance. She had her arms crossed and he wanted to say she was being petulant for the sake of it, but he saw in her eyes what he felt.

Bone-deep worry. And bone-deep exhaustion.

"It's a lead to follow," Palmer said gently. "Better to be wrong about it than not check it out."

"Your brother's sending a group out this way, but by no means everyone," Hawk said, his voice void of any inflection. It seemed to be something he *extra* put on for Anna. "No doubt when the FBI get here, they'll want to look into this lead too."

Anna let out a little growl of distaste, but she didn't argue any further.

Palmer focused on the satellite and GPS and instructed Hawk where to drive and then where to stop. It wasn't surprising the property wasn't used for anything. It was mostly rocks leading up into mountains. There was some tree cover around, but even the somewhat flat ground was mostly rocky.

"No fence," Hawk noted. "I could just keep driving. But it's going to bang up your truck."

"I don't care," Anna said. "Get us as close as you can."

Hawk nodded and turned the truck off the road. It was bumpy and Palmer had to grip the door handle and grind his teeth together to keep from making any noise of pain.

But *damn* that hurt.

"You see that?" Hawk asked, pointing in the distance out the windshield. Palmer leaned forward, trying not to grab his side in pain. But he did see it. It looked like rocks, but not like the mountains or boulders. More like a structure.

"Drive toward it."

Hawk nodded and moved forward, though he had to slow the pace given the rocky ground. Palmer could only be grateful. Much more jolts to his gunshot wound and he might just pass out.

"Better stop here," Hawk said. "There's still some cover in case we've got company."

Palmer and Anna nodded, and Palmer studied the structure from inside the truck. It was half in the earth, half out. A kind of cellar that wasn't fully underground. It had a door, but the windows were just holes in the stone, not glass.

More concerning than this creepy building was that there were remnants of a campfire, not lit but still smoldering right outside the open door.

As if on cue, Hawk and Anna pulled guns out. Anna handed Palmer one. They didn't even have to communicate getting out of the truck. They did it in unison, coming together and standing in kind of a back-to-back triangle while they each surveyed the world around them.

Palmer was breathing a little heavily from the pain in his side. Sweat had even popped up along his forehead. But this was a lead and he had to follow it through.

"Maybe you should stay put," Hawk offered, no doubt concerned by Palmer's huffing and puffing.

"Maybe you should mind your own business," Palmer returned through gritted teeth.

"What do you think?" Hawk asked Anna.

She was quiet for a beat of silence, all three of them scanning the horizon for signs of people.

"We could leave him, but he won't stay put. So he might as well be with us."

"All right. Someone's clearly here or been here very recently. We don't know if it's who we're looking for, if it's dangerous or how many people we might be up against," Hawk said, clearly taking charge. Palmer was all right with it in the moment—he was busy trying to stay upright. The surprising thing was that Anna didn't seem to argue with him for the sake of it.

Because, for all of them, the important thing was finding Louisa.

"I think it'll be a good fifteen before Jack's people get over here, but I don't think we should wait," Anna said. "Every second counts."

"Agreed. We'll head out," Hawk said with a nod. "See what we can find, but we've got to stick together until we've got more information. We've got to work as a team. Understood?"

"Yeah," Anna said. "Understood."

Palmer nodded because he didn't trust his voice. The good news was that even if the pain wasn't subsiding exactly, he was closer to having a handle on it. On not huffing and puffing and feeling like his whole body might give out.

"Let's search the building."

They moved forward as a unit. Hawk opened the door while Palmer and Anna held weapons to cover him. Then they entered in a line and quickly returned to their tactical positioning.

The building was empty. No rooms to hide in or things to hide behind. There was a chair in the middle of the room, and some ropes and a blanket on the floor.

Palmer's stomach tensed like a fist. Someone

had been held here against their will. He didn't want to say that out loud, but he supposed he didn't have to. It was clear.

"She was held here," Anna said flatly. "Clearly."

"There's no evidence Miss O'Brien was here. There's no evidence that rope was used to tie someone to that chair," Hawk pointed out. "It could very well be unrelated."

"It's a reasonable leap," Palmer said, though his voice was rough—and not because of pain. At least, not physical pain. All too well, he could picture Louisa tied to that chair. All too easily, he could think of all the terrible reasons she wasn't anymore.

"You can't make leaps like that in an investigation."

"Maybe not in an arson investigation," Palmer replied. "But in a cold case, you've sometimes got to make the leaps that lead you to a new direction to go in."

"This isn't a cold case either," Hawk noted. "It's an active investigation."

"We've got lots of different teams working different angles to find Louisa," Anna countered. "So, we'll take this angle. We'll assume she was held here. By at least two people, maybe three. We follow all those prints outside and see what we can find. I'm an expert tracker."

She was already moving back out of the building, and Palmer watched as Hawk struggled with some inner argument before following her. Palmer then followed him, and Anna was already studying the prints.

"A struggle of some sort?" Palmer asked.

Anna crouched down and looked at the prints more closely. Most were just a mess of indents in the snow, but there were a few clearer ones. "There's one that I'd say is a man's boot," she said, pointing to one. "Much larger than the others. But… I can't really tell the others apart. There are an awful lot of prints, and they're all kind of the same size. There are some differences in tread, so I can tell we've got at least two others besides the man. I took some pictures at the original site."

She pulled out her phone and opened her photos. Then held it up against the largest one. "I think this might be the guy who shot you, Palmer." She held the phone so Hawk and Palmer could look and compare.

"I think you're right," Hawk said, "which means we're on the right track."

"These prints aren't frozen over either," Palmer said, crouching and making an *oof* sound in an effort to hide the groan of pain. He poked at the snow around the imprints. "But those are," he said, indicating the more uniform ones. "We can guess that those are from last night or even yesterday, and these less clear ones are from today." He squinted up at the sun. "Because they haven't had a chance to freeze over."

Though it grated, Anna took his arm and helped him to a standing position. Hawk looked at him speculatively.

"It doesn't matter if I'm up to this or not," Palmer said to him, though Hawk hadn't *expressed* any of his obvious concerns. "I'm not resting till she's found. It doesn't have to be me, but I can't sit around and wait."

Hawk didn't react to that in any way. He looked back down at the tracks. "I say we follow those. I assume that's what you want to do?"

"It's a miracle. You actually assume right," Anna said, keeping her arm linked with Palmer's like he needed the support. "Jack's guys can follow us. If we get into a scrape, they'll get us out."

Palmer figured she was speaking with more confidence than she felt—Lord knew it was more confidence than he had. But what else was there to do? They could hardly sit around and wait when it was clear Louisa had been held against her will.

With no discussion, Hawk took the lead, followed by Palmer, with Anna holding up the rear. They were careful to follow the tracks without disturbing them, so it was clear which ones were the search party's and which ones were the perpetrators'.

It was already pretty confusing because there were multiple people involved. Anna was an expert at tracking and even she couldn't tell some of the footprints apart.

They didn't move quickly. There were a lot of reasons, but they all annoyed Palmer. He didn't want to be careful. He didn't want to give a thought to the excruciating pain in his side.

He only wanted to find Louisa.

But he wanted her alive, so the tactical slowness would have to do, no matter how his impatience strained.

They started to climb rocks and Hawk and Anna switched places since Anna was better at tracking. But this was hard, because without the snow, she could only track places there *was* snow or different inconsistencies that she could only guess were tracks.

They stopped for what felt like the hundredth time as Anna crouched and studied a little area of snow. "Two people went this way." She poked at the snow, then looked up at the direction she must think the tracks went. "But at different times."

She straightened, did a little circle around a large rock. Then she pointed in the opposite direction. "Then two people—two different people, because the boot tracks are different—went this way. Together."

"Which one's Louisa?" Palmer demanded.

Anna inhaled, frowning. "It's hard to say. Three of the tracks are almost exactly the same size. Slightly different treads on one of them. If I'm making those big leaps I'm not supposed to make in an investigation, I'd say Louisa is the one with slightly different treads and there are two women, likely, with the same boots, working with the gunman." She pointed to the first direction. "Which makes me think maybe Louisa got away, ran off. Then someone followed. Hence, why they were hiking at different points in time. The other two people?" She shrugged. "I don't have a clue why they'd go in a different direction."

"We should split up," Palmer said.

Both Hawk and Anna looked at him dubiously. "Only if by 'splitting up,' you mean you go back to where we were and wait in the truck until the search party gets here, and Anna and I follow Louisa's tracks."

Palmer scowled. "Not on your life, bud."

"Then we stick together. Anna will…" He trailed off, frowning. He looked around, but all Palmer saw was blue sky. Then he heard… something. He glanced at Hawk, who nodded. He'd heard it too.

They all held completely still, listening to the

sound. Almost like voices. Hawk made a hand motion to follow him, so Palmer fell into step behind him, Anna behind Palmer. They moved so slowly, it could hardly count as movement, but it kept them from making any noise and helped them continue to listen.

The voices had stopped, but there was still a sound. Like a rustle. Palmer followed Hawk, step by careful step, as they rounded a boulder.

Hunched over a bag in a little clearing between rocks was the man who'd shot him. He had a gun in one hand, his other hand in a canvas sack. His back was to them, and Palmer didn't think he'd heard them.

Hawk drew his weapon and stepped forward, so Palmer and Anna did the same, flanking Hawk just in case.

"Drop it," Hawk ordered.

The man did not drop his weapon, but he looked over his shoulder at them. He eyed Palmer with some surprise. "Thought I'd killed you."

Palmer did his best to look like the gunshot was nothing. He stood on his own two feet, kept his grip on the gun firm but not tight, held the man's glare. "Thought wrong."

"You've got three guns on you," Hawk said, almost conversationally. "It's in your best interest to drop yours."

"Is it?" He jutted his chin above them. Palmer

didn't look, afraid it was a trap, but he heard Hawk and Anna swear.

"Got a sniper up there," Hawk muttered.

The guy who'd shot him smirked, still crouched there next to a bag. "You shoot me, the girl here gets it," he said, pointing at Anna.

Since Anna and Hawk each had an eye on a gun, Palmer scoped out the area around them. So far, just this guy and their sniper—who wasn't that far up the mountain. From Palmer's vantage point, she looked young. Younger than Anna even. She wasn't quite dressed appropriately for the Wyoming winter, but she held the gun with clear comfort and adeptness. The scope was trained right at Anna's head.

Anna was still, but mostly appeared unfazed. She met his gaze and raised an eyebrow. An old sign. In any other circumstances, he might have laughed. But this wasn't some bar after the rodeo where Anna wanted to start or finish a little trouble—with his help.

This was life and death.

He shook his head at her, but she rolled her eyes. A clear sign she wasn't going to listen. So he knew he had to wade in. Just like always.

Because, five seconds later, Anna leaped forward and tackled the guy on the rocky ground, the sniper fired and all hell broke loose.

Chapter Twenty

Something nudged Louisa out of the odd pseudo sleep she'd fallen into. Not a real sleep. There was nothing restful about it, but exhaustion and boredom had taken over, so she hadn't fully realized her eyes were closed.

And then jerked open because something… Something had happened. Something had changed.

She kept her body very still. It was hard to see since inside the cave was dark and outside was blindingly sunny. She willed her eyes to adjust to the contrast. She listened, or tried to listen, but her heart was echoing in her ears and it was hard to hear beyond that.

When she couldn't take it anymore, she took a deep, careful breath and then slowly and quietly let it out. When she moved, she did so slowly and carefully, but still she'd grown so stiff—not just in her ankle or side, but all over—it took a great effort not to let out any kind of noise of pain.

She closed her eyes in an effort to focus and just remember that she could survive any temporary pain if she could get out of this. She'd escaped that cellar, so survival was an option. She just had to be smart.

When she reopened her eyes and gave them time to adjust, she moved her body again, this time taking into account how much every muscle ached. She tried to account for her injured ankle in the small, cramped space.

When she finally managed to maneuver so that she could see outside the cave opening, she was sweating and her breaths were coming in short pants.

Temporary pain, she chanted silently to herself as she peered out the opening into the sunny afternoon.

She didn't see anyone or anything. The sky was still blue and the sun higher than it had been, but still not yet late afternoon. So she hadn't been here, half asleep, that long.

She listened for the sounds of anyone, or even an animal, but didn't hear anything. Until someone spoke. Loud and clear.

"You shouldn't have run, Colleen."

Louisa recognized Kyla's voice, but she didn't see her. Was Kyla talking *to* her or just to herself as she searched for Louisa somewhere nearby? There was no way to know since Louisa couldn't see her.

There was the faint sound of something small and light falling. Pebbles. They tipped over the cave opening and onto the ground at Louisa's feet.

Kyla was above her. Louisa tried to look up but the sun was too bright and the overhang of the cave too thick.

"Come out, Colleen. I know you're in there." More pebbles fell as Kyla shifted above her.

Louisa figured it was better to emerge while she could, hiding her injured ankle as best she could, and giving herself more means of escape rather than be stuck in the cave. But Kyla definitely had the high ground. Still, Louisa turned to face off with her, even if she had to squint against the sun that seemed to shine down on Kyla standing on a boulder above the cave, gun in her hand.

"My name is Louisa," Louisa said firmly, hands curled into fists. Okay, she couldn't fight off a bullet, she couldn't even run at this point, but she could fight. "Louisa O'Brien."

"Your name is Colleen Brown," Kyla said, her finger curling around the trigger of the gun. "You're the reason my life has been hell. I was going to wait. I was going to make her pay. You ruined the plan. You ruined everything, just like always." She shook her head, and there were tears in her brown eyes. "I'll just kill you both. I'll just kill us all."

But she didn't point the gun at Louisa. Louisa used her peripheral vision to get an idea of where she could jump or hide if Kyla did. It would hurt, but there was a spot she could lunge for that would give her some cover.

For now, she looked at this woman and tried to figure a way out of this without any shooting. "Why, Kyla? Why should anyone die? I'm your sister. I thought you reached out because you wanted family. I could be your family."

Kyla stared at her. She shook her head sadly. She was crying now, and Louisa honestly didn't know how to play this situation. "I had a plan," Kyla repeated. "You always ruin the plan."

"Okay." Louisa nodded even though she knew the plan was her being *murdered*. Kyla looked more disheveled than she had last night. Like she was unraveling along with all her plans. "You had a plan. It didn't work out quite the way you wanted it to. That's okay. That's life."

"What do *you* know about life? You got everything. I was left with *nothing*," Kyla snapped. Whatever grasp she seemed to have on control was slipping. The girl was crying harder now, and again Louisa felt a sliver of sympathy for her. Even as Kyla's grip on the gun tightened.

"You don't have nothing," Louisa said, though

her throat was tight with both fear and sadness. "Because we're sisters. That could mean something if you let it. But not if you kill me. Then you really do have nothing. It'll all be over. And you'll end up paying the price. It doesn't have to end this way."

"If I showed her... If I proved to her that I was the better daughter. That she was wrong about me. About my dad. Then it would all be okay." She wiped her tears and running nose on her sleeve. "But it was never okay because of *you*. He was only hard on everyone because of *you*. She only left everyone because of *you*."

Louisa felt torn because this was just sad, heartbreaking really. She wanted to reach out for the girl, help her. But without a plan, with all this emotion, Kyla was even more unpredictable. Even more dangerous. "Kyla," she said, trying to sound calm, trying to hold Kyla's off-and-on stare. "Killing me doesn't change anything."

"She'd pay. She'd finally pay."

"But if our mother... She set up the whole kidnapping thing like you said, because I wasn't your dad's—" Louisa didn't know if she believed Kyla's story, but she knew it best to act as though she did "—but she didn't kill me. She didn't try to find me. She...gave me up, I guess? I don't matter to her. She threw me away."

"Don't you see?" Kyla demanded. "You matter

the most. She got you out. She knew. She knew what he was. What he'd do. But I had to stay. I had to make it all work. She saved you. She sentenced me."

"I'm sorry," Louisa said, and she felt her own tears threatening. "I am so sorry for whatever you've had to go through, Kyla. I *am*. But it didn't have to do with me. You have to see that."

"Why do I have to see that?" Kyla replied, lifting the gun a little, not fully pointed at Louisa, but close enough to be a problem. "If you hadn't been born, if you hadn't been given up, everything would be different."

"Different isn't always better."

Louisa moved a little to the left, trying very hard not to make her limp noticeable. Kyla's finger was still on the trigger and the gun hadn't moved from that too-close-for-comfort position. If Louisa had enough of an idea of when she'd shoot, she could jump out of the way.

Oh, it would hurt. She'd likely break something, but it would be better than being shot, wouldn't it? Of course, Kyla would probably just follow, shooting again. So it was a temporary solution to a long-range problem. What other choices were there?

Before she could decide—or Kyla could decide anything, for that matter—there was a shout from not too far off. Followed by a gunshot. It all distracted Kyla enough that Louisa could limp behind a boulder.

Maybe someone had come to help. Maybe she was free.

Either way, she had to do what she could to make sure Kyla couldn't kill her. She hobbled over the rocks, ducking behind them to create as much of a shield as she could. Before, she'd climbed up the mountain thinking that would be escape, now she went down. If someone was out there, someone had come to find her, she could get to them.

She could get to safety.

She skidded down one flat rock and had to take a little leap. She focused on landing on her good foot, but the force of it nearly injured that one too.

Somehow she managed to stay upright. There was pain, but not the same kind of pain that was in her other ankle. She moved to the next boulder, kept working her way down. It was the only chance to survive.

She didn't know if Kyla followed or was heading toward the shouts and gunshot. It didn't matter. All that mattered was getting down. Finding someone who could help.

Louisa's entire body was shaking, and she lost her balance once, enough to kind of roll down a boulder. She tried to fall at least somewhat strategically, but in attempting to keep from hurting her ankle any more, she left the rest of her body unprotected and her temple slammed far too hard into the edge of the boulder as she came to a skidding stop.

She didn't shout or scream in pain. She was already in too much agony for that to really penetrate. But she felt something kind of sticky run down her forehead and lifted her hand to try to wipe it away before it got into her eyes.

It was blood, of course. Hell. She could not afford this on top of everything else. She wiped as much from her forehead as she could so it wouldn't impact her eyesight. But of course it was a head wound, so it just kept bleeding.

She looked around. She'd fallen into a spot between rocks, and as long as Kyla didn't come from straight up, Louisa might be able to hide here out of sight if she stayed low.

At least for a little while. At least until help came. Help had to be coming.

That's when she heard something. Footsteps, grunts. The sound of flesh and bone hitting flesh and bone. Gunshots. She rolled onto her stomach and peeked through the opening between two rocks to see if she could find the source of the sounds of a fight.

Because a fight had to mean help.

Down below was a clearing, and she immediately saw Anna's blond head. Anna was crouched behind her own rock, while the girl who'd been working with Kyla shot from a higher position across the clearing from Louisa. Hawk was fighting off the man who'd shot Palmer with punches and kicks. Two guns were on the ground around them and they both seemed to be fighting to keep the other from reaching them.

Then she saw Palmer. Alive. God, he was *alive*. She nearly wept right there. He held a gun, was pointing it at the girl on the rise. He was alive and here and…maybe it could all be all right.

She heard footsteps behind her and knew she had to brace herself for Kyla before any of them could be considered safe.

PALMER CURSED HIS shaky hands. He didn't want to take a bad shot, but the sniper just kept firing off rounds at the rock Anna was huddling behind and, from his position, he couldn't get a good angle on the shooter—even if his hands were steady.

Anna had lost her gun in the skirmish. After she'd launched herself at the guy, and the sniper had missed a few shots, Hawk had waded in and taken over, while Palmer had shoved Anna behind the rock she was currently behind.

There'd been a near miss from the sniper and he'd had to dive behind his own rock rather than help Hawk disarm the man on the ground. Not that Palmer had much of his usual fight in him, he knew. Hawk was holding his own, and as long as the fight went on, the sniper couldn't risk taking a shot at Hawk without shooting her own guy.

They needed to take that sniper out, but Palmer could not find the angle he needed.

"Would you hurry?" Anna shouted at him.

"Can't. Need a better angle." He surveyed his surroundings one more time. He needed higher ground but getting there would put him out in the open, not to mention be more of a struggle than he'd like with his injury. Maybe—

He saw the flash of movement up above, out of the corner of his eye. He immediately whirled, thinking it was a threat, before he realized he recognized that coat, that black hair. He almost shouted, but at the last moment, he understood she was alone. Hidden.

She had to stay that way, but he needed Anna to know she was there.

Because Louisa was alive. Right *here*. Safe in her little alcove of rocks. The relief was so potent, his legs nearly went to jelly.

"I can take her out," Anna yelled at him, bringing his attention back to the problems at hand. "Toss me the gun," Anna said, gesturing at him.

Tossing the gun was a terrible idea, but Anna had a better angle and, if she took out the sniper,

Palmer could get up to Louisa. He looked at the sniper's location one more time, then Anna's, and fired in the general direction so the sniper would duck.

He used that break to run like hell across the way to Anna. He skidded to a stop just as another gunshot exploded around them. He pressed the gun into Anna's palm, ignoring the stabbing pain in his side that was thankfully yesterday's pain, not a new gunshot wound. "Take her out if you can, but no matter what, keep covering me. Louisa is up there. I'm going after her."

Anna looked up at the rocks above them. Then swore. "She's not alone."

Palmer didn't think, not about the sniper or the guy Hawk was fighting. He just took off, doing his best to scale the rocks even as his body screamed at him to stop. Even as gunshots and shouts sounded around him.

He reached Louisa almost at the same time the other woman did. Looking so much like Louisa, Palmer finally realized what this was.

"You're Kyla Brown," he said, firmly placing his body between Kyla and Louisa. Because Kyla had a gun and Louisa was already bleeding. So much blood on her in fact, he couldn't focus on anything but the attacker or he'd fall apart.

"And you're the interfering boyfriend." Kyla

pointed her gun at him. "Weren't you already shot once? I don't need you. I'd happily shoot you again. Step out of the way."

Palmer only spread his arms, as if that alone could shield Louisa. He'd do anything. Play human shield. *Anything.* "I can't let you kill her."

Kyla shrugged. "Then I'll just kill you both."

Louisa tried to push around him, but Palmer only grabbed her and held her back, still hidden behind his body. She looked up at him, the blood smudged all over her forehead causing his stomach to cramp.

"Let me go," she said. Her eyes full of tears. Her face bruised and scratched and pale. She was favoring one leg and her clothes were torn.

"Like hell," he replied.

She huffed out a breath and pulled far enough away from him that she could look at the woman and speak.

"Kyla. It's over. If you put down the gun, no one has to die. And you can... We can get you the help you need. It'll be okay. I promise you. I will do everything I can to make this okay."

Kyla shook her head. She had her finger around the trigger, the gun pointed in their vague direction, though she didn't seem to be aiming. The girl seemed more desperate and devastated than determined to gun them down.

She wasn't as beat up as Louisa, but she'd undoubtedly been crying. She was clearly lost.

"It'll never be okay," she said. "You ruined everything."

Palmer saw the moment when Kyla just gave it up. He knew what was coming. He jerked Louisa to him, hoping he could get them both out of the path of the bullet, but using his body to shield Louisa regardless.

The shot rang out, loud and far too close. It echoed in his ears, but there was something… odd about how it sounded around them. How he didn't feel that slice of pain. Was it shock? Had she missed?

He looked down at Louisa, running his hands along her body. Surely the bullet hadn't gotten to her. "You're okay?"

"Yes, I… Palmer." She pointed behind him.

Kyla was on the ground. Behind her crumpled form was Jack. He was already moving forward for Kyla's gun, which had clattered to the ground. He had his radio pulled to his mouth and was shouting out orders.

Louisa pushed around Palmer and rushed forward to Kyla.

Palmer noticed her limp and followed with some errant thought that he would carry her away. He would do anything to get her away from all this.

But she knelt next to Kyla, who lay on the ground. Kyla wasn't dead, because she was kind of crying and making an odd whining sound, but not writhing around exactly, which was a concern.

Jack knelt on her other side and pulled something out of his pocket. Ironically, Kyla seemed to have been shot in almost the exact place Palmer had been.

"Will she be okay?" Louisa asked Jack.

Palmer didn't know how she could be worried about this woman when Kyla had literally just been about to kill her, but he rubbed Louisa's back and didn't say anything while Jack answered.

"We've got medics on-site. It'll be rough getting all the way up here, but everyone's doing their best. They found Hillary Brown, Kyla's mother, tied up in the truck of a car not far from here. She also needs medical attention. As does the sniper Anna took out and the man Hawk beat up."

"She deserves to die," Kyla said between gritted teeth. "Mom. Colleen. They all deserve to die."

"Who's Colleen?" Jack asked, looking up at them.

"Me," Louisa said, her voice just a croak. "I'm apparently Colleen Brown."

Jack sent Palmer a quizzical look but didn't question any further. There'd be time for that yet. The medics crawled up the rock face and took over. Palmer pulled Louisa away from Kyla. He wanted to carry her down to the ambulance himself, but he wouldn't be able to hack it.

"Louisa needs a hospital too," Palmer said to Jack once Kyla had been taken away.

"Yeah, so do you," Jack replied. "You would have been dead if I hadn't shot her."

That was probably true. Maybe the first gunshot wound hadn't killed him, but likely the second would have. If it would have saved Louisa... He'd choose it a million times over, but...

He had Jack. "I guess it's a good thing I've got a big brother looking out for me."

Jack heaved out a breath. "What kind of recklessness would ever make you think it's a good idea to run an escape mission twenty-four hours after being shot?" he muttered. He didn't wait for an answer though. He moved away and began shouting orders at people below.

Meanwhile, Palmer held on to Louisa while they waited for the more pressing injuries to be looked at.

"I knew you had to be okay," she said into his chest. "I knew you all would come. I knew it."

He pressed his mouth to her temple. "Always, Lou."

Chapter Twenty-One

Louisa was taken to the hospital with Palmer. Hawk and Anna were given on-site treatment but hadn't needed to be transported. All of Kyla's crew, including her kidnapped mother, had.

Louisa supposed in some strange way, Hillary Brown was her mother, but she just couldn't… grasp that. The problem was, she didn't know how in touch with reality Kyla had been. Had anything she said been true?

At the hospital, Louisa had been checked out and patched up. She had a brace for her sprained ankle, a few stitches in her forehead and some concussion protocol. She sat in a room, waiting for the all clear to go home, which was supposed to be coming.

Police came in and out. At the point she was just about ready to yell at her next visitor, Mary ushered her family into the room.

They were all crying. Even Grandpa. That made her cry too. They huddled around her, and Louisa realized that, no matter the truth, she was so lucky. Because this was her family.

"We don't understand this story, Louisa," Dad said. He looked so tired. He'd been through too much. The house fire, now this.

"Let me go get Jack for you," Mary said, offering a smile. "He should be able to explain some things better."

While they waited, Mom fussed with Louisa's hospital bed. Grandpa and Dad paced and Grandma settled herself in the chair and pulled her knitting out of her purse.

Louisa was certain, no matter what the actual truth was, they hadn't *kidnapped* her. They weren't those people.

After a few more minutes, Jack came in. He was in his uniform, and no doubt had been up for over twenty-four hours straight. She'd heard from various people how many people had gotten together to look for her—not just the police departments, but townspeople and her own family. She'd heard how Anna had busted Palmer out of the hospital before he was supposed to go, how even Hawk Steele had worked to help find her.

She had this whole community that cared about her, which made it just…really hard to hold on to any anger toward poor Kyla Brown.

"We tracked down Janice Menard," Jack explained after greeting her family. "She didn't talk, but Birdie Williams did when we explained that a lot of this went down on her property. She claims she wasn't involved, and so far the evidence backs that up, but Janice was, and Birdie shared what she remembered."

He told the story in quick, concise facts, making sure to meet the gazes of her parents and grandparents. Louisa knew Anna and Palmer both complained about Jack, even while they hero-worshipped him in some respects, and she fully understood that in a way she hadn't before.

For all the times he could be rigid and interfering and overbearing, he excelled at this. Giving people in trouble and trauma what they needed.

"Along with the nurses we've talked to, Hillary Brown has confirmed a lot of this story," Jack continued. "She faked a kidnapping of her infant child because she was afraid of her husband finding out the baby wasn't his. She worked with a nurse, Janice, who she knew through her brother, to create a kind of baby-swap situation. Her baby would go to someone who'd just had a baby, and that infant would be left with family services."

Mom gripped Louisa's hand so tightly it hurt. Louisa didn't say anything. She just gripped her mother's hand right back.

"Are you saying my baby…?"

Jack crossed over to Mom and put his hand on her shoulder. "Birdie explained that, unfortunately, your biological baby was stillborn. Instead of telling you that, Janice simply put Louisa in her place."

Mom let out a shaky breath.

"It seems Kyla Brown has been planning this for some time. Some initial investigation, and some of Kyla's own statement, indicates she had found proof of this and was blackmailing Janice to help her get to you, Louisa. Hawk is leaning toward Janice being the prime suspect for the fire, at Kyla's directive." Jack looked around the room. "This is a lot to take in," Jack said. "We're still collecting details. While we are, I'd encourage you all to take care of yourselves. Answer law enforcement's questions as best you can, and trust us to clean up this mess. We'll be coordinating our efforts with all agencies involved to make sure all the culprits are brought to justice."

Mom nodded dully, still clutching Louisa's hand.

"I know you're waiting on the doctor to let you out, Louisa, but if your family doesn't mind, I'd like to take you over to Palmer's room." He gestured to the wheelchair in the corner. "If I don't take you to see him, he's only going to bust out again, and he needs to stay put."

Louisa looked up at her mother. Not so much because she needed permission, but she needed to know her mom was going to be okay.

Mom smiled, though it wavered. "You go on. We'll get everything ready so we can take you back to Grandma and Grandpa's as soon as you're released."

Everyone worked together to help her out of the bed and, even though she insisted she could walk with some help, everyone insisted harder that she use the wheelchair.

Eventually, she gave in. Jack wheeled her from the room and over to the wing Palmer was in.

"Can you tell me if she's okay?" Louisa asked once she'd braced herself for whatever answer there might be. "Kyla."

"She'll make it. There will be a psych eval. An investigation into her mother. The man who shot Palmer?"

Louisa nodded.

"That was her father. We already knew he had some priors, but it looks like he's got some aliases too, that might have even more warrants. The young woman who was working with them is connected to him in some way we're still untangling. So, everyone's going to survive, be investigated and checked out, and we'll work to make sure all the outcomes are the best for everyone."

"Thanks, Jack. I…" She sucked in a breath. "You…" He'd saved her life. Oh, it had been a joint effort, she knew, but he'd been the one on that rise. Because the Hudsons were just…built that way. To run in and save.

"I'm sorry this all happened," Jack said gravely, stopping in front of a door she figured was Palmer's. He crouched down so they were eye to eye. "And we didn't get to you sooner."

She knew he meant that, and that no doubt it brought up some memories of his parents' disappearance, for both him and Palmer. That made her feel a guilt she knew probably didn't belong on her shoulders. But if she hadn't asked for Palmer's help… "I'm sorry I dragged Palmer into it."

"I imagine he dragged himself just fine," Jack replied. He studied Louisa for a long minute. "I know he seems to think I see him only as a screwup…"

"That's because you treat him like a screwup."

"Fair enough."

"You could change that, you know."

Jack stood, clearly done with *that* line of discussion. "I'll see what I can do."

PALMER EYED THE IV in his arm and the door. There'd been enough hubbub that he'd finally found himself alone in this dang hospital bed.

So he'd needed a few stitches redone, and to be pumped full of antibiotics, and blah, blah, blah. He hadn't lost consciousness again, so wasn't that something? He was just fine.

And he needed to see Louisa.

She was here somewhere, so he didn't have to sneak out of the hospital. He could even take the IV tower with him. He just had to time it right. In between nurse visits and his family descending on him like a plague of locusts.

He was staring at the clock, trying to determine that perfect timing, when his door opened. He didn't see anything at first, except Louisa.

She was in a wheelchair, a bright white bandage on her forehead, but her green eyes were clear and direct. Because she was okay. They were both okay.

Something that had been bound around his chest for the past two days finally lifted.

Then he realized Jack was the one pushing her wheelchair, still in his uniform, and he came to a stop so Louisa was pointed right at Palmer in his bed.

"Visitor. Can't stay forever because she's getting sprung before you," Jack said. "If you don't stay put, I'm going to make sure you never have a visitor again."

Palmer managed to look away from Louisa and up at his brother. The man who'd saved his life and then, with everything he had going on as the sheriff, had thought to bring Louisa to him. "Thanks, Jack."

Jack nodded. "I'll just go check on some things." He left without so much as a lecture. That truly *was* a gift.

Then Louisa was stepping from her wheelchair. He reached out in some dumb attempt to stop her. "Hey, you shouldn't be getting up."

She didn't stand long. She scooted into the bed with him. "I'm fine. They just don't want me putting weight on my ankle for a while. Nothing broken, just a sprain. So this will work." She wiggled in next to his good side and he slid his arm under her neck as she rested her head on his shoulder.

She let out a contended sigh. Then turned her forehead into his shoulder. "I was so afraid you were dead."

"Same goes, sweetheart." He pressed a kiss to the top of her head and held her close. "But we both made it out okay, so I guess we're stuck with each other."

She huffed a little laugh and he was glad he could lift her spirits, even if it was temporary.

"They're saying that what Kyla said was true."

"Yeah," Palmer said, stroking his hand down her hair. "Jack filled me in. You okay?"

"I don't know. I guess I feel more sorry for my mom than anyone."

"She's a strong lady. You all will get through it. They love you no matter what, Lou. You'll all find a way to deal."

She inhaled deeply. "Yeah. I think so. I just… I guess I feel sorry for Kyla too."

"She was going to kill you," he said flatly. Because Kyla almost had. So easily. In those twenty-four hours they couldn't find Louisa, Kyla could have done anything. So many bad outcomes could have happened, and he wouldn't have been there to stop it.

"She wasn't well, and I don't think anyone ever gave her a chance to be. I just hope she can get the help she needs."

"Well, I'll hope for that too then." Because he wanted Louisa to have whatever she wanted, however she wanted it. All he wanted was for Louisa to be happy, and she had a lot of complicated stuff to wade through. So if this would ease some of that pain, he wanted that for her.

It was a lot to come to terms with, even if they'd uncovered a lot of it before Kyla had taken her. But he still had a question. "There's just one thing I don't understand. What was your grandpa doing skulking around when we were investigating? You were suspicious of him, but he didn't have anything to do with this."

"He said he was trying to hide Grandma's Christmas present and was mad because he thought I was stealing his hiding place."

Palmer chuckled then winced, because he'd refused the heavy-duty pain meds so his side *hurt* now that the local anesthetic was wearing off from the redone stitches.

Louisa snuggled closer. "You're in pain."

"Those painkillers just make me fuzzy."

"They help you rest and heal." She lifted her head and glared down at him. "Next time the nurse comes, you're taking something."

He didn't know why it struck him then, when she was glaring at him, with that terrible bandage on her head and her hair a mess and him in pain a thousand times over, but he just…was so glad she was there. In his life. In his bed… even if it was a hospital bed.

He reached up and tried to smooth some of her tangled hair down.

"Okay." And maybe that *okay* should have been an *I love you.* But he didn't want to say that under the harsh hospital lights. With her head bandaged up and him in a hospital bed. He wanted something…better.

For her.

For both of them.

Epilogue

Christmas dawned snowy and cold. In some ways, it was a bit like the Christmases of Louisa's childhood. She was in a house with her parents and grandparents. They ate breakfast, opened presents.

No one spoke of what had happened, but there was a different weight to the day. A gratefulness that might not have been there otherwise. Because, despite all that had happened, they were so incredibly lucky to all be all right and all have each other.

In the afternoon, Dad and Grandpa drove over to the orchard to check on things while Grandma and Mom discussed and bickered a bit about dinner preparation plans. As she always had, Louisa retreated to her gifts and appreciated the normalness of it all.

It was all she wanted from here on out. *Normal*.

Until she saw through the living room picture window Anna's truck pull up. And Palmer get out. Then she didn't want *all* the old normal things.

Louisa grabbed her crutches and, against Mom's and Grandma's admonitions, snatched her coat and went outside.

"Do not go down those stairs, young lady. You let him come to you," Grandma called out the door.

She would have listened, but she didn't even get the chance because Palmer was already jogging over and up the stairs.

"Whoa, whoa, whoa. Too snowy for those crutches, Lou."

"Are you supposed to be driving?" she demanded.

"Doctor gave me the all clear."

She studied him, looking for a sign of a lie, but he seemed to be telling the truth. "Did you bring me a Christmas present?"

He grinned down at her. "I'm your present."

"That's ridiculous. Even for you." But she wrapped an arm around his neck, her other arm holding on to the crutches. He was on the mend and here and...

It wasn't like all the pain of the past had magically been cured, but she was okay. Her parents and grandparents were okay. There was pain.

There was confusion, but at the end of the day, what held them all together was love.

Because it didn't matter that someone else had given birth to her. It only mattered that her parents had raised her and loved her.

She'd met with Hillary Brown a few days ago. There'd been no real connection there. Louisa couldn't say she wanted one, and the woman was even less interested.

Whatever issues Kyla had, they'd at least partially come from a very troubled family life that, in a strange way, had very little to do with Louisa at all. It wasn't easy to let that go, but she was working on it.

And there was Palmer. Every day. Just…there for her, in all the ways she needed him to be.

"Come on. I'll take you for a drive if you let me help you to the truck. I already cleared it with your mom."

"Did you?"

He offered his arm and she went ahead and left her crutches behind. Because wherever they drove, he'd be there to help her. It was very hard to feel sorry for herself with all this upheaval when she had so many people in her life who rallied around and helped.

He got her into the truck and then drove out toward the Hudson Ranch. He didn't say much. Asked what she'd gotten for Christmas and the like, but he was otherwise uncharacteristically quiet. Even as he pulled onto what she knew was Hudson land, but more on the west side, farther away from the main house.

She didn't ask where they were going. He seemed to have some kind of plan. He took the truck off road, then pulled to a stop in a pretty little clearing. It was a Christmas postcard. Untouched snow and pine trees, the mountains in the far distance.

He didn't move to get out, just stared through the front windshield. "I was thinking about building a place out here. This is my share. Nice place to have a house, don't you think?"

She studied his profile. He was being very… odd. She figured that's how she knew it was important. So, she looked out at the spot. It was pretty. It'd be a nice quiet place to have a little spot. Private enough to feel like your own place, but close enough to the main house it would be his.

"It's perfect," she agreed.

"Probably take a while but, you know, eventually." He finally looked over at her.

He was just so handsome. So…hers. "Eventually," she echoed.

He smiled, shook his head and let out a gusty sigh. "Lou, I love you."

She let it sink in. Really sink. Into all those

places so convinced he never would or could. Palmer Hudson loved her. Yeah, she was a lucky woman.

"Well?" he demanded when she didn't say anything.

She just smiled up at him, really enjoying the look of confusion on his face, even if it was a little mean of her. "Well what?" she replied.

"Aren't you going to say it back?"

She pretended to think about it, because he looked so out of his element and it wasn't every day someone could make Palmer out of his element. Might as well enjoy it. "I might just let it sit awhile."

He stared at her, completely and utterly speechless, for a good full minute. Until she couldn't hold her laughter back any longer. Palmer Hudson loved her and was talking houses and eventually. With *her*.

"I love you, Palmer." And she had, for a very long time, but this was more than that. Not just a feeling, kept deep inside. But something shared, that they'd work on together.

She leaned across the middle console and pressed her mouth to his. "And I like the sound of eventually," she added when she finally pulled back.

He grinned at her. "I should hope so. I did take a bullet for you."

She rolled her eyes, but she liked him back to himself. "I was wondering how long you'd wait to pull that card."

"I'm not really sure I've gotten an adequate thank-you," he continued. "I'm basically your personal hero," he added.

"Yeah, you are," she said, far more serious than he was being. Even as she reached over and kissed him again.

Because he was her hero, and he always would be.

* * * * *